Walter's Searchlight

a novel by Anderson Hobbs

Pat —
Thank you for reading
and sharing
this story.
Follow the light!
—Andy Hobbs

For my family and especially C.V.A. Sure do miss you, pal.
— A.H.

ISBN: 978-0-9910624-0-9

"There, but for the grace of God, go I."
— English proverb

This time, I mean it

Time stood still the moment I first saw my child. In those frozen seconds before baby Lilly cried and opened her eyes, I witnessed the meaning of life. Exactly ten years later, my daughter sends me over the moon and brings me to my knees, sometimes in the same breath.

I wonder if my father thought the same of me. I miss him, but I'm glad Pops can't see the way I live today. I am one big bundle of disappointment, wrapped in shame and tied together with regret. If I could turn back the clock and make better decisions, I would.

I take full responsibility for hurting my baby girl. All I want to do is make things right. Like my father, I'm not perfect, but I will do the best I can. I will set an example for my daughter and prove I am more than what my failures suggest. I will fix what I broke, or die trying. This time, I mean it.

- Walter's latest journal entry

--

Walter Wadsworth was homeless.

He stepped off the bus in downtown Lakehaven with his brown leather satchel and vinyl garment bag. He walked a block to the Shady Acres Motel, his white shoes crunching shards of broken sidewalk glass that sparkled in the sunset.

Crushed beer cans and crusty condoms littered the motel grounds. By the chain-link fence was a television with a hole shot in the center. Next to the TV sat a pile of yellow-page phone books, soaked by months, maybe years, of that steady Northwest drizzle.

The motel lobby reeked of garlic and fish. With water dripping from the lid of his white baseball cap, Walter rang the front desk bell in the rhythm of "shave and a haircut, two bits." The manager emerged from behind a red velvet curtain.

"You need room?" the Asian lady asked.

"Do you have any clean rooms available?"

"All rooms are clean, very clean," she said. "You need room? Fifty-nine dollar."

Walter handed her two twenties.

"This not enough," she said. "Fifty-nine dollar only, or no room."

"Ma'am," Walter said. "I will pay you the rest tomorrow morning. You have my word."

She recognized Walter and smiled. Last month, he had stayed one weekend. He didn't cause trouble like the pimps and drug dealers.

He showed the manager a wallet photo of his ten-year-old daughter, Lilly.

"They grow up too fast," he said. "She's a big fifth-grader now."

"Aw, she very pretty," the manager said. "She have your big eyes and big smile."

"Good thing she didn't inherit the mustache," Walter said. They laughed. With more small talk, he learned that both of their daughters attended Mount Rainier Elementary School. The manager gestured to a portrait of her daughter on the wall, and Walter said she looked like a sweet girl.

The manager looked at the wallet-sized photo and tilted her head. "I bet you such good father," she said.

"I try my best," Walter said. "I don't get to see my baby girl enough." He swallowed and struggled to maintain composure.

"Tell you what," the manager said. "You can stay two night for price of one. You pay me next time. Deal?"

"Thank you, ma'am," Walter said, reaching out to shake her hand. "You're an angel."

With the key in hand, Walter prayed the room was clean. He shuddered at the thought of the worst room in the complex, where a middle-aged couple on welfare had lived for two decades. Their room smelled like dead laundry. The couple had a decaying station wagon with handicapped plates. The car was stuffed with boxes and clothes. Patches of green moss dotted the hood and caked the car's crevices.

Walter's room was four doors down from the office. The locker room aroma slapped him in the face as soon as he opened the door. Walter tossed his satchel and garment bag on the faded floral bedspread. The yellowed curtains had soaked up years of dust and cigarette smoke.

Walter had one hour before he was allowed to pick up Lilly. He gulped a pill, grabbed his brown leather satchel, locked the motel door and hoofed it toward the bus stop. Walter's head got heavy in minutes. The setting slowed. Narcotic relief coursed through his veins and cemented a toothy grin on his black face.

Every time Walter visited Lilly, the anticipation was a drug. He remembered the pitter-patter of her feet on the hardwood floor when, as a toddler, she would run full speed and crash into his legs with a bear hug.

Walter craved those hugs.

The bus stopped at the street where his main antagonist lived. Her name was Rose - Lilly's white mother and Walter's ex-wife. Rose had purchased a three-bedroom house in a middle class neighborhood. The modest gray rambler had a two-car garage, a wraparound porch, wide windows and a lone evergreen in the front yard. The place mirrored Walter's last permanent address, the one he had shared with Rose. Motels, buses and sofas kept him transient ever since. The first time he had seen Rose's clean-cut house in Lakehaven, he was crippled with shame. That's when he began to accept, inch by inch and day by day, that he was homeless, perhaps for the rest of his life. The shame of letting down his daughter through divorce, however, was a shame that never subsided. This emotion guided his behavior, for better or worse.

Walter was thirty minutes early for his scheduled visit with Lilly. The house was dark and his knock went unanswered.

They must be running errands, he thought. He sat on the wooden steps leading to the front porch. He leaned back on his elbows and listened to the traffic from the main thoroughfare in the distance. To the south, downtown Lakehaven glowed from the ground up, defying the dusk.

Walter checked his watch. It was now twenty minutes past their scheduled time. He walked three blocks to a convenience store pay phone and called Rose's cellphone. No answer. Walter relieved himself in the store's restroom, then bought two single-shot bottles of whiskey on his way out.

"I need some condoms," Walter said.

The clerk gestured to the Trojans on the back shelf.

"No, not those," Walter said, pointing to the right. "I need The Magnums."

"Um, do you want large or extra large?"

"Large," Walter said, winking. "I like a tight fit."

A rain-soaked Walter returned to the quiet house, where visitation should have started an hour before. Inside his satchel was a white envelope, which he tucked inside the screen door. Inside the envelope was a birthday card with a

4

pink fairy wishing his daughter a happy birthday. Inside the card, Walter had written:

Lilly, you light up my life. I love you, baby girl.
Love, Daddy

Walter went to the graffiti-laden pay phone and called Candy, then returned to the Shady Acres Motel. He found Candy idling in a pickup truck, parked across from the room beneath a flickering street lamp. The redhead stepped out, wrapped in a sweatshirt and tight jeans with a stitched pattern on the back pockets.

Candy changed in the bathroom. Her clothes rustled behind the green door as Walter peeled off his wet jacket, sweater and jeans.

"Are you ready?" she said.

"Come on out and let me see you." Walter sat on the edge of the bed and opened the whiskey bottles.

Candy stepped out in high heels and a see-through teddy. Walter's wide eyes gobbled her figure.

"Candy ... you ... are ... beautiful," he said as she twirled. Walter's striped boxers formed a tent.

For a mature hooker, Candy's skin defied age. It was smooth and healthy, with only a hint of sag, although she applied a liberal layer of makeup to her heart-shaped face. Walter gazed at Candy's red toenails, then worked his way up. One hand rested on her hip, her long fingers spread apart, her nails with chipped red polish. She flicked a short whip in Walter's direction, reached over and snatched a whiskey shot from his hand. They clinked bottles and drank. She hand-cuffed Walter to the bedposts and whipped his groin.

The next day marked the beginning of Walter's rise to fame in Lakehaven.

First impressions

Walter the homeless man wore a black three-piece pin-stripe suit. The leather satchel hung from his slender six-foot frame. He smelled like cologne and armpits.

Fresh from the bus stop, he entered City Hall through a revolving door. The Lakehaven School Board met in the council chambers. Frustrated parents filled the seats.

He signed up for public comment, then watched from the back wall.

At the school board meetings, public comments were limited to three minutes. A yellow light blinked on the lectern when the speaker had ten seconds left. A red light and a buzzer signaled that time was up.

The school board president, flanked by six more white-haired Caucasian school board members, announced that it was Walter's turn to speak. Walter approached the podium and cleared his throat. His masculine honey-dipped voice flowed through the sound system.

Good evening, citizens of Lakehaven and the Lakehaven School Board. I am honored for this opportunity to speak to all of you.

I am a new resident in your school district, but I am

no stranger to its shortcomings.

I am shaken by the low test scores from black students, especially the boys. Parental involvement is only half of the solution.

The school district's slogan is 'Diversity matters.' A slogan is nothing without action. The district struggles to understand what diversity means, as evidenced by these disheartening test scores.

In today's politically correct society, we are not allowed to say that Lakehaven is failing because of all the brown kids. Many of these brown kids have no father at home. Sometimes they go to bed hungry. Sometimes the family car is their bed.

I am here today, not on behalf of minority children, but on behalf of all children. The children of Lakehaven deserve a good education. Knowledge is power, and these children need all the power we can give them.

What I want to know is, will you help me? Or will you stand back and admire the district's diversity from a distance?

Our children's future is at stake. Please heed the call.

Heads turned and whispered to one another, asking if anyone knew the name of the black man who just spoke. A lone middle-aged man in the audience, however, stood and clapped with conviction. That man's name was Joe Lippy, and many in the audience rolled their eyes at Lakehaven's outspoken school critic as he applauded.

Walter left the council chambers before the next citizen took the podium, and Joe jogged after him.

"Hey!" Joe called to Walter, who was crossing the shaggy lawn toward the bus stop.

Walter met Joe with a hearty handshake and name exchange. The streetlights made shadows of the men on the lawn. The Puget Sound breeze chilled their faces.

"It's good to finally meet someone who isn't drinking the education establishment's Kool Aid," said Joe, his wispy gray hair whipping in the wind.

"I have a daughter in these schools," Walter said. "It's in my best interest to know what's going on."

"We have a lot to talk about," said Joe, and they laughed. "I'm a retired math teacher who survived three decades of the school district's bullshit."

"Say, Joe, would you mind giving me a lift to the bus station? I've been walking all day. My feet are throbbing."

"Sure," Joe said. "My car's over here."

In the corner of the parking lot was Joe's white Volkswagen Rabbit. One rear wheel was missing a hubcap, and the windshield had a foot-long crack across the driver's side.

"That was an excellent speech you gave in there," Joe said, shifting into first gear. "You should get it published in The Searchlight."

"That crossed my mind," Walter said.

"At one time, I wrote for The Searchlight every Sunday, but they cut me off," Joe said. "The editor and his bosses always succumb to pressure from the status quo, you see. The local media get cold feet about printing the truth."

Joe slowed down at the stop light. Walter climbed out with his satchel and thanked his new friend for the ride.

"Talk to the editor about your speech," Joe said. "You really tell it like it is."

Walter walked two blocks to the Shady Acres Motel and hunkered down in his dusty room.

He swallowed another Oxioid and plopped on the bed. Before passing out, Walter gazed at the picture of Lilly in his wallet. He heard a man and woman argue in Spanish in the adjacent room. Walter tuned out their voices with the television, which coated his room in a blue haze. The wall and the headboard rattled behind Walter's head in rhythm to the couple's coitus. He drooled on the pillow and his eyeballs rolled beneath their lids.

He dreamed about riding the bus to the Asian massage parlor. The bus expanded to a dance floor with flashing technicolor tiles. A mirrorball hung on a string from the ceiling, rotating at an Earth-like pace. Throughout the dream, the sound of a tuning fork rang in his ears. A nude madame bent over, put both palms on the floor, then rested her knees on her elbows.

"Punish me, Daddy," she said, licking her red lips. Walter swatted her ass with the leather paddle. Instead of a swat, he heard a thud. He swung the paddle and it thudded again.

The third swing snapped Walter awake. He opened his eyes and saw the water ripple in a glass on the nightstand. He heard a commotion outside, and someone pounded on the neighbor's door.

"Lakehaven Police! Open up!"

Walter panicked. He reached around and felt a lump on the back of his head, which was sore from inside to outside. He vomited in the trash can. Police pounded on the neighbor's door - bam! bam! bam!

"This is your last warning!" yelled the officer. "Answer the door or we'll knock it down!"

Groggy and stumbling, he grabbed the orange prescription bottle and fumbled with the lid. Walter was a black man with a full bottle of Oxioids, caught up in a police raid at a motel for criminals.

The officer pounded on Walter's door.

"Lakehaven Police. Open the door."

Walter stood barefoot in his boxer shorts and T-shirt. He put the orange bottle in his mouth and slobbered all over it. He reached into his boxers, spread his butt cheeks, and winced as he wedged the pills into his cavity.

The officer knocked again.

"Lakehaven Police. Open the door."

Walter waddled across the room, opened the door and stuck his head out.

"What happened, officer?"

"Sir, there was - holy shit! Are you all right?"

The back of Walter's head was bleeding. Blood trickled down his back, neck and shoulders. A framed painting had fallen on the bed, at the same spot as Walter's sleeping head. There was a hole in the wall where the painting had once hung. The hole came from the neighbor's shotgun.

The shooter, a suspected pimp and drug dealer, was gone before police arrived.

"I didn't see anything officer," Walter said, holding his hand over the back of his head. "I went to bed early."

"Sir, would you like me to call an ambulance? That gash looks painful."

"Yes, I would appreciate that," Walter said, the pill bottle still lodged in his ass. He envisioned a clean hospital bed with three meals, cable TV and sexy nurses.

"Stay right here, sir. I need to speak with the motel clerk," the officer said. He jogged over to the office with the red vacancy sign flashing in the window.

Walter hobbled to the toilet, sat down and pushed like a man. In less than a minute, the orange bottle was washed, dried and stuffed into the brown satchel where it belonged.

At the hospital, the X-ray revealed no major injuries, much to the astonishment of the young doctor, who wrote Walter a prescription for painkillers.

Two hours later, Walter had another orange bottle, just in time to meet his daughter after school.

Smart like your Daddy

Walter waited for Lilly outside Mount Rainier Elementary School.

"Daddy!" she said, running with arms outstretched and her pink backpack bouncing on her back. She buried her head in his chest and wrapped her arms around him and squeezed with all her might.

"How's my baby girl?" Walter said, patting her back in a rhythm with both hands. She looked up, and his mustache tickled her forehead when he kissed her. "How was your day?"

"It was awesome!" she said, jumping up and down, her belly jiggling in a pink sweater. "I got a peppermint candy. See?" She showed him the half-dissolved red-and-white-striped sucrose disc on her tongue.

"How did you get that?"

"I got all my multiplication tables correct."

"Right on! That's my girl. I'm glad you have a teacher who prefers teaching over baby-sitting," Walter said.

Walter wrapped his arm around Lilly, and they walked down the street to Sub King for a snack. The transition to autumn was evident in the colored leaves and chilled air.

"Remember our game with the math problems?"

"Yeah!" Lilly said. "What's the square root of sixteen?"

Walter scratched his chin stubble. "You tell me."

"Four!" Lilly said.

"What's ten times ten?"

"One hundred."

"What's the square root of sixty-four?"

"Eight."

"If x plus one equals three, what is the value of x?"

"Two!"

"That's my girl!"

They ordered a pair of assembly-line hoagies on bread fresh from the oven and sat at a corner table by the window.

"I'm glad you're going to this school," Walter said, crunching on a potato chip. "Do you like it so far?"

"Sort of," she said, holding a tuna sub with both hands. "I sort of miss my old school."

"Your new school has more white kids."

"Why?"

"Because it's in a white neighborhood," Walter said. "All the money and resources go to the schools where more white people live. Simple as that."

"Why?"

"No one wants to teach at a school where all the kids speak Spanish and are only there for the meals."

"Lots of kids speak Spanish at my school."

"At other schools, that's the only language the kids speak."

"It's a good thing I speak English, right?"

"Yes, dear," Walter said, laughing. "You'll be fine."

"Daddy, do you know why I do so well in school?"

"Because you're smart like your Daddy," Walter said. They laughed.

"Yeah, and do you know why else? Because we work together on my homework."

"That's right." Walter coached Lilly on math, sometimes

only for a few minutes, but it kept them sharp. "So how are things at home?"

"Fine, I guess." Her expression went neutral.

"What's the matter? Something wrong?"

"If I tell you something, do you promise not to get mad? Do you promise?"

"Lilly, I'm your father, for crying out loud. Just tell me."

"Mom said we might move to Spokane."

"Spokane? You just moved to Lakehaven," Walter said. "Why Spokane? Why now?"

"She wants to get a job there or something."

"Did she get any offers?"

"I don't think so," Lilly said, shrugging. "Sometimes she talks about moving to Spokane, but I don't want to go. I'll miss you."

"Don't you worry about a thing," Walter said. He reached across the table and nudged her chin with a knuckle. "I won't let my baby girl get away."

At the motel that evening, Walter revised a journal entry to print as a letter for The Searchlight. He expanded the speech he had delivered to the Lakehaven School Board. He challenged parents to take the math portion of the Washington State Student Assessment Test and see how they stacked up against their own children:

> Students are taught to take tests. Teachers shape classroom material around these tests. And students, mostly students of color, fail these tests.
>
> Neither the teachers nor the students are to blame. The culprit is the test itself, written by white educators for white students, ignorant of today's cultural framework. We are stuck with all the wrong answers until we ask the right questions.

Lakehaven bus station

The next morning at the Shady Acres Motel, Walter woke up before the sun. He dressed and grabbed his satchel.

"Baby, where are you going?" Candy said, eyes half-open, groggy from a night of spanking and dog leashes.

"I'll be back with coffee. Any other requests?"

"Oooh, get one of those iced cinnamon rolls by the cash register," she said.

Minutes later, he backed out the convenience store doors with two hot styrofoam cups and a plastic bag. Out of the corner of his eye, he saw a white minivan at a red light, ready to turn toward the freeway exit that was spray-painted with a silver anarchy symbol. He set the coffee and cinnamon rolls on top of a metal Searchlight newspaper box and dashed up to the van, pressed his palm against the passenger side window and expected to see Lilly.

Inside the van, two white teenagers screamed at the big black man who tapped on their window. The van's wheels screeched through the red light and onto the freeway.

Walter was as calm as a surgeon. He ditched the cinnamon rolls and coffee, and walked toward the bus station a block away, making a mental note to call Candy later. He found a concrete bench at the terminal and hid behind a dry edition of The Lakehaven Searchlight, which he held with out-stretched arms. Walter gazed at the newspaper's gothic-script nameplate with a lighthouse between the words "Lakehaven" and "Searchlight."

The Searchlight was named after a defunct lighthouse on Lakehaven Bay that overlooked the Puget Sound from a rocky leg of land. The rustic lighthouse was the city's only historic landmark. Once upon a time, before Seattle expanded its ports, the lighthouse guided boats and barges through the fog and darkness. The lighthouse was located in the so-called nice side of Lakehaven.

About a mile from those upper middle class neighbor-hoods was the not-so-nice side, where the motels and police sirens co-existed among the seedier frequencies of Lakehaven's heartbeat. The freeway split the city in half. The map failed to show the rich-poor divide. Well-heeled professionals on the west side of the freeway commuted to Seattle. On the east side, the pimps and gangbangers and perverts and rogue immigrants kept the cops busy. The middle class was the real minority, sprinkled throughout the city limits.

The skyrocketing real estate prices in Seattle had pushed poor people to the suburbs, and Lakehaven was the region's unofficial poster child for suburban poverty. This bedroom community of 100,000 people had evolved into a haven for strip malls and immigrants in search of cheap rent. Nowhere was this more evident than in Lakehaven schools. In schools on the east side of the freeway, more than half of the students received free or reduced-price lunches. Two elementary schools taught lessons in Spanish.

While parked on a bench, Walter scanned the front-page headlines, including a piece on suburban poverty in the Se-attle area and the burden on Lakehaven's school district. The report noted that ten percent of Lakehaven households spoke no English. A quote from a social worker said it all:

"If ten percent of Lakehaven children can't speak English, then ten percent of students won't learn diddly squat."

He smirked at a front-page teaser for a report on Lakehaven magnate Theodore Rosewater's charity ball, then turned the page to crime news.

"Woman beaten by her pimp," he said, reading the police blotter headline out loud. "As opposed to what?"

The cold rain patted the bus shelter and traffic splashed across the asphalt. The station bustled in the morning. Giggling Korean teenagers sloshed across the parking lot to another terminal. A steady stream of briefcases and umbrellas passed in front of the benches. In the twilight hours, the benches doubled as beds. The bus station in Lakehaven attracted a rough crowd at night, although the buses themselves were generally safe. Walter was mugged a few weeks before. A black teen had pulled a gun on a wasted Walter and demanded his wallet. He remembered the hangover better than the robbery. The first sight of the teen's gun had frightened Walter to the core. He wanted to see his daughter grow up. He handed over the wallet with sixty-four dollars. The teen disappeared in the darkness.

Walter held The Searchlight in both hands. The newspaper ink tinted his chilly fingertips. Overcast skies hid the morning sun and failed to trap the morning chill. The air ignited Walter's nose and lungs.

He turned the page. One crime entry involved an ex-lover and a machete. Another reported the sexual assault of a ten-year-old boy in a hot tub. Crimes against children infuriated Walter, who clenched his teeth while reading that particular news brief.

Another story in The Searchlight examined the aftermath of a local tragedy. One year ago, a U.S. Marine mailed a death threat to the president and held his elderly neighbor hostage.

Secret Service agents surrounded the Lakehaven Heights Apartments in minutes. The Marine wore a bandoleer of bullets across his body and booby trapped the apartment unit. He had served eight years in Iraq before a medical discharge for post-traumatic stress disorder. He shot the elderly woman and himself as the SWAT team entered.

One year later, lawmakers in Olympia narrowly passed tighter regulations for the purchase of military-strength ammo by civilians.

Walter folded the newspaper and tucked it into his satchel, then boarded a bus to Seattle. He had a doctor's appointment and hoped to score a new prescription.

"How are you, my friend," he said, shaking hands with a homeless man in his mid-twenties who sat in the back row. "How many?"

The guy held up three fingers. Walter fished inside his satchel for three tiny white discs. Each pill was stamped with a number fifteen.

Walter collected thirty dollars. He made another four hundred dollars total on the bus trip, hanging out at a handful of stops along the way. The money was spent by midnight.

--

Divorce had set Walter on the path to drug dealing and homelessness.

A few years back, Walter had sweet-talked his way into an appointment to the water commission in Everett. Trouble began a month later. The new intern was an angel and a devil at once. She pranced like a fawn in a field of daisies, flashing a contagious smile for anyone who said hello.

Walter salivated when she squatted in front of the filing cabinets. Her thong panties peeked through her thin skirts. She complimented anyone who wore stripes, and whispered about anyone who dressed out of tune.

It was the intern's first day. She reported to Walter, ready to fulfill his clerical desires.

"Hey there, boss man," she said, coiling hair around her manicured finger.

"What brought you to the Northwest?" Walter asked.

"My best girlfriend scored a j-o-b and, like, needed her best girlfriend to come too," she said.

"Anything I can do to help in your adjustment, just let me know," Walter said, handing her a stack of applications. "Can you take care of these background checks this morning?"

"You got it," she said and winked.

After a month of lunches and flirting and long walks around the building, they agreed to meet at a dive bar, somewhere outside the office happy hour circuit.

They met at the Sidetrack Saloon. They picked the most level billiards table in the place and racked up the balls.

"I'm such a flirt when I play pool," she said. "I can make you mess up."

"We'll see about that," he said, cracking the flat pyramid of balls. The striped nine-ball rolled into the far corner pocket. She swayed closer, slid her fingers along his shoulders and whispered "good luck" in his ear. She pressed her palms to the table's edge and leaned forward, giving her cleavage room to breathe. She nibbled his ear. He could have smacked the cue ball with his erection.

Two beers and two games later, they migrated to the driver's seat of his white wife's black Cadillac.

His wife found out about the affair when the intern called the house. Rose kicked him out and moved with Lilly from house to house, living like suburban nomads until settling in Lakehaven. Walter followed in a bus. He befriended the local motel managers.

One weekend after the divorce, Walter had taken Lilly,

who was clad head to toe in pink, to a carnival in a parking lot. Downtown Lakehaven reeked of corn dogs, trash and carnival workers who needed a bath.

With four tickets each, Walter and Lilly boarded the Tilt-a-Whirl, her favorite ride. They spun like tops in the rusty bucket seats. Walter laughed like she'd never heard him laugh before. Lilly and Walter laughed and laughed and laughed. The Tilt-a-Whirl slowed to a stop.

"What next?" Walter asked. "You hungry?"

"Can I have some cotton candy?"

"You got it, baby girl."

"Yeah!" said Lilly, clapping her hands. "Daddy, can we go on the merry-go-round?"

They rode side by side as the horses bobbed up and down, rotating in sync with a calliope tune.

"Daddy, can I have a hot dog?"

"You sure can."

"Yeah! Daddy, you're the best."

"We need to catch the bus soon," he said. "It's almost time to take you home."

That night, long after bedtime, Lilly was startled awake. She grabbed her teddy bear and scampered into her mother's room, where Rose slept alone in a double bed. Lilly crawled into bed on the empty side where the sheets were cold, and rested her head against Rose's warm back.

That night, long after exchanging goodbye hugs with his daughter, Walter caught the all-night bus known as the Motel Express. The driver turned out the lights.

Walter's eyes filled with tears as he pressed a cheek against the cold window glass.

Thank you for
reading The Searchlight

The presses hummed all day and all night at The Lakehaven Searchlight. The metallic ink permeated the building,
and during hot weather, the aroma was intoxicating.

The Searchlight occupied the northeast corner of Foster
Street and Commercial Avenue, a short walk from the bus
station. The newspaper building was divided in two. During
the day, the office side bustled as marketing reps sold ads and
journalists wrote the news. After midnight, the presses and
delivery trucks ruled the building.

The editorial department was housed in the west wing,
where the newsroom decayed from the inside out, the walls
and ceiling tiles stained by years of leaking water. Duct tape
patched the torn spots on the industrial-strength carpet.

In addition to general neglect by its corporate owners, The
Searchlight hung in legal limbo as owners pitched the paper
to potential buyers.

For a small daily newspaper in Seattle's shadow, The
Searchlight was a formidable competitor and champion of the
people. In the 1990s, the paper exposed a statewide scandal
over a mismanaged subsidy account for alternative fuel vehicles. The accounting glitch had cost taxpayers millions.

Walter Wadsworth approached the receptionist's desk and

asked for the editor, Ernest Handsy.

"Do you have an appointment?" asked the receptionist.

Walter nodded and stared at her cleavage. "I apologize for being late. I don't want to keep him waiting."

She pressed a white button on her desk that unlocked the door to the editorial department.

"His office is in the back," she said, avoiding eye contact with Walter, who smelled neither sweet nor sexy.

"Thank you, ma'am," Walter said, tipping his white baseball cap. "You have a good day."

Ernest sat behind an L-shaped wooden desk that had years of scratches and nicks. Lining three of the office's four walls were stacks of newspapers standing three feet tall. Every two stacks contained one year of Searchlights. The stack closest to the desk was the most yellowed stack, and the yellowed papers faded to white as the eye followed the newspapers around the office. A Lakehaven map spanned one wall.

Walter stood in the editor's doorway and knocked in the rhythm of "shave and a haircut, two bits."

"Yes, what can I do for you?" said Ernest, standing up to shake hands. The bespectacled editor, with a barrel chest and full gray beard, stood five feet six inches tall. His belly strained the buttons on his starched white shirt.

"I'm Walter Wadsworth," he said, taking off his white hat. "I was told you could print a letter about our schools."

"Of course, have a seat," Ernest said. "You must be the same Walter Wadsworth who gave one hell of a speech at the school board meeting."

"You heard about it?"

"I hear about everything in Lakehaven," Ernest said.

Walter handed the editor a sheet of ragged-edged paper ripped from a spiral notebook. Chicken-scratch cursive in blue ink covered both sides.

Ernest set down his plain white coffee mug and reached

for his eyeglasses. Ernest flattened the paper and followed the words with his finger. With a red pen in hand, the editor asked for clarification when he could not read Walter's writing. The impromptu task took a bite out of a busy morning at the newspaper.

"Looks good," Ernest said, taking off his glasses. "We'll get your letter in the hopper."

"Thank you," Walter said. "Listen, I really need you to print this on Saturday's opinion page."

"It all depends on what space we have available," Ernest said. "I'll do what I can."

"Ernest, please," Walter said. "This is an urgent message for the sake of our city's children of color."

Ernest didn't have a problem saying no, unless it was to black people like Walter.

"I'll find a good spot for it," Ernest said, standing up for a firm, equal-ground handshake. "Thanks for writing."

Incidentally, the letter ran on Saturday's opinion page, next to an editorial that praised the school district for its ethnic inclusiveness. Gossipers and gadflies called Lakehaven's education watchdog in residence, Joe Lippy, wanting to know more about Walter.

"I agree with Walter Wadsworth's assessment of the school district's failure to educate minority students," wrote one reader. "Thank you for having the courage to print the truth."

--

That afternoon, after his first meeting at the newspaper, Walter met Lilly outside school at the usual time and place. The rest of the children stormed out of the building at the final bell. Lilly walked with her head down, lagging behind the crowd.

"What's the matter, sweetheart?" he asked.

She burst into tears and buried her face in Walter's chest. He held her and rubbed the back of her pink sweater.

"These boys always make fun of me at lunch," she said, wiping tears from her chubby cheeks.

"What do they do?"

"They tease me about my weight. They saw me getting another hamburger at lunch. Now they say 'Hey Miss Piggy' or they make pig noises when I eat." She wiped another tear with the heel of her hand, and sniffled. "Everybody's laughing at me, Daddy."

"Are they in your class?"

"They're fourth-graders."

"How long have they been doing this?"

"It started this week. I just want them to go away."

"Baby girl, don't you pay any attention to those fools," Walter said. "They're trying to get a reaction out of you. Don't give them what they want."

"Mom said to ignore them, but now they do it more."

Walter paused for a moment. The school grounds were clear as the last few teachers walked to their cars.

"Let me tell you something," Walter said, wiping her tear with his thumb. "You are a beautiful and smart girl who will grow up to do great things, and by then, you won't even remember the names of those two assholes."

"I hate those assholes."

"Watch your language, baby girl," Walter said. "Do as I say, not as I do."

They walked two blocks to Rose's house. Lilly munched on peanut M&M's that Walter brought for her. In the driveway, Walter hugged Lilly goodbye for the day.

"Mmm, I love you," he said, playfully squeezing hard. "I want to squeeze you until your head pops off."

"But Daddy," Lilly said, laughing at their little ritual. "I need my head."

23

He smothered her with one last barrage of kisses, and she jogged toward the front door, smiling.

"Bye, Daddy!"

"I love you, baby girl!"

That night, upon returning to his musty room at the Shady Acres Motel, Walter wrote his first official guest column for The Searchlight. The next morning, he barged into Ernest Handsy's office unannounced and insisted that the editor read the handwritten ragged-edged pages.

"Walter, I'm impressed," Ernest said, setting the pages down and removing his glasses. "Let me ask you - would you be willing to write regularly on Lakehaven education issues? We have a slot on Saturday's opinion page."

"I can do that," Walter said. "It's about time The Searchlight had a black columnist."

"I'll even type up your handwritten masterpieces," Ernest said. "There's one other thing we need."

"What's that?"

"Your picture."

Ernest snapped one photo of Walter that morning.

"You look like a million bucks," Ernest said. "Like a true old-school newspaperman."

The column ran the following Saturday, with a picture of Walter in a white shirt collar and black tie.

What would Martin Luther King do?
By Walter Wadsworth, Searchlight columnist

Fellow parents, I am frustrated.

Just like you, I want a quality education for our children. Just like you, I want Washington schools to receive adequate funding from the state.

Cities with lots of brown students, like Lakehaven, are relegated to the back of the proverbial school bus - if the bus even picks them up in the first place.

Ethnic minorities comprise more than half the student population in Lakehaven. That is not an excuse for poor performance on state reading and math tests, even if those tests are written through a Eurocentric worldview. That is a discussion for another time.

Throwing money at the education problem will halt the symptoms, but won't cure the illness.

Success for children starts and ends with parents. A child without parental support in education is like a child trying to paddle across the Puget Sound in a paper cup with a plastic spoon for an oar.

Education is merely a tool. Schools are simply workshops. Teachers are stretched to capacity. It's up to parents to supplement their children's education. Parents must equip their children with the confidence to harness those educational tools and succeed.

There is no simple solution, but there is a simple first step. Parents, please turn off the television and the Internet and the video games and the iPods. Now put a book in your child's hands. Better yet, read with your child.

Of course, if I had a magic wand, all children would eat three meals a day, wear clean clothes, kiss both parents goodnight and sleep under a dry roof.

But let's get out of La-La Land. The reality is that for some families in Lakehaven, basic survival is the paramount duty. There are transient families who focus not on test scores and homework, but on their next meal. One cannot truly understand such hardship unless you've walked in those shoes. I have walked in those shoes.

Regardless of economic disparity, all kids need a strong family foundation with sure-footed parents. This foundation forms the bedrock of a child's conscience and fosters an ability to self-motivate.

I have a daughter who attends school in Lakehaven. While I may fall short of parental perfection, I am committed to doing my part in molding her young mind. For encouragement in this category, I suggest we ask one important question: What would Martin Luther King do?

Dr. King's leadership and passion taught America a lesson in fear. The essence of the Civil Rights Movement was to erase fear between races and foster harmony among all. Dr. King held a mirror to society, and society saw the ugly truth. Because of Dr. King, segregated schools are a footnote.

When holding a mirror to education in Lakehaven, I see untapped potential. I see a willingness to succeed. I see parents who stand behind their children, dedicated to helping them grow.

Sadly, the school district's declining student achievement is like a plant that wilts from a lack of water. The key to education is growth. Let's stop the wilting in our schools. Let's nourish our children with the skills and knowledge to thrive. The solution starts, and ends, at home. Let's help our children grow.

As we begin this daunting journey of rebirth, I am reminded of a quote from Dr. King: "Faith is taking the first step, even when you don't see the whole staircase." Lakehaven schools are at a crossroads, and the road ahead is dark. I am ready to move forward, motivated by faith, powered by hope, and guided by love.

Poison apples

Walter sought tips from Joe on persuasive writing as they rode to the school board meeting in the Rabbit.

"Writing an essay is like building a house," said Joe, exhaling a cloud of pipe smoke while shifting gears. "Before you start gluing together all the pieces, make sure you have all the pieces. You need to grab readers by the throat, balls, heartstrings, or all three. You should almost be embarrassed when you write, you see. That's when you know it's good."

Walter nodded along to Joe's lecture. The Rabbit splashed through several rain-filled potholes, bouncing the men in their seats. Walter saw an obese granny who sat in a wheelchair at the bus shelter, reading The Searchlight.

"Teachers in Lakehaven need to teach these kids how to write with purpose," Joe continued, "instead of making the kids circle nouns and verbs on a worksheet."

The world outside Walter's head slowed down considerably on the ride to City Hall. Walter had gobbled two Oxioids and was headed to La-La Land.

Walter planned his route to the upstairs men's restroom. He wanted water and a place to vomit.

"I'll meet you in a minute," Walter said.

Walter trudged up the stairs to the men's room that was

overpowered by pine-scented cleaner. He splashed cold water on his face and drank from the faucet. He ripped a sheet of paper towel from the dispenser and blotted his face.

Walter went downstairs and into the council chambers, where the school board members and audience had stood for the Pledge of Allegiance. Walter watched in the doorway, his right hand flat on his chest. As everyone sat down, Walter weaseled his way to the empty seat in the back row.

The first commenter of the evening was Joe.

"These low test scores are inevitable because we're afraid to hurt the feelings of the kids who fail," said Joe, who ran a hand through his gray mad scientist hair. "The willingness to fail is the only way to learn. How can these children learn if we don't let them fail? Once upon a time, when you competed, there was one trophy, and guess who got it? The winner! And guess what everyone else got? Nothing!"

The red light buzzed.

"I guess that's all the time I get," he said, slapping his palm on the lectern. "Someone ought to run for school board and change the limit for public comment from three minutes to five minutes."

Walter paid closer attention to staying awake than listening to Joe's speech. The school board members said nothing. When Joe's time was up, the board president called the next citizen's name, and Joe returned to his seat.

After public comments, the board discussed a proposed policy for eliminating traditional letter grades - A, B, C, D, F - and replacing them with a pass or fail mark. Joe and Walter had already left.

"Bus station?" asked Joe as they drove out of the parking lot. "I can drop you off at your place. Where do you live?"

Walter paused. "Right now, the Shady Acres Motel," he said, looking at his shoes. "My ex-wife moved with our daughter to Lakehaven. That's the main reason why I came to

Lakehaven - to see my daughter."

"Have you been looking at apartments?" Joe asked.

"This motel living won't last forever. Just for now."

In front of the office at the Shady Acres Motel, the red neon vacancy sign reflected off the Rabbit's hood.

"I hate to ask for one more favor," Walter said, "but can I borrow twenty dollars until payday? I'll pay you back."

Joe fished a worn black leather wallet from his back pocket, then handed Walter a crisp twenty dollar bill.

"I appreciate this," said Walter, shaking Joe's hand before stepping out of the car. "Bless you, brother."

About fifteen minutes after gulping an Oxioid for a nightcap, Walter sprawled on the motel bed with a notebook and pen. In blue ink, he scratched the title "The Poison Apple of Education." He ripped out the page and threw the wadded paper across the room. He rested his spinning head on the floral-print bedspread and fell asleep with his father on his mind.

The last time Walter saw his father was at his college graduation. Walter was the first in his family to finish. On the way to the ceremony, he rolled joints on his flat cap, then blazed with a car full of white college buddies. One of those guys went on to sell cars, one became a high school gym teacher, one joined the Marines.

Walter's graduation was itself a miracle. "C equals Commencement," he would say.

Walter missed the maximum amount of classes possible. If he would have put as much effort into his studies as he did trying to get out of them, he would have made the Dean's List. Walter's typical strategy involved sweet-talking the professor into giving him an all-or-nothing assignment - and he'd ultimately pass the class. Walter had a gift for creating his own clean slate.

In the gymnasium, after the grads had tossed their caps and filed out the door, a short and stout man with a gray beard waited for Walter. He wore an ironworkers union shirt with red suspenders clipped to faded blue jeans. One thing caught Walter off-guard, and that was his father's gap-toothed smile. His father rarely smiled.

"I'm proud of you, son," said Walter Sr., thumbs hooked on his belt loops.

"Thank you, Pops," said a very stoned Walter, surprised at his father's praise.

"Son," said Walter Sr., the smile disappearing. "What are you going to do now?"

Walter shrugged his shoulders.

"Son, what are you going to do with your life?"

"Pops, I'll figure it out."

"You better figure it out."

"When did you figure it out?"

"Son, I figured it out too late."

Joe Lippy's new pal

Joe tutored Walter in the ways of the school board meeting, which doubled as an orgy for the gadflies.

The public comment period was their time. These bored grumblers flung every idea against the wall, week after week, month after month, year after year. Most of the public comment was civil. Everyone wanted to hear what the crazy bunch said next. Joe spouted failure rates like they were the Lord's Prayer, doused in sour rhetoric.

Joe and his new pal, Walter, guided the gossip with a choker leash.

On this particular evening, Joe bitched about flip-flop sandals, and whether they should be allowed in schools.

"The students, especially the boys, shouldn't be looking at the girls and their feet," he said, pounding the podium. "They should be studying math equations and literature, not feet. This is a serious distraction to proper learning. Painted toenails are causing Lakehaven's young men to make babies and flunk out of school. When will you people wake up?"

Joe shifted to the dismal test scores in Lakehaven.

"According to Education Magazine, 73 percent of black students are failing," Joe said at the lectern. "Did you know that the number of Lakehaven students on free and reduced lunch is fifty percent? How can children learn anything when they're hungry? And why don't teachers teach these kids how to eat right? All this junk food and energy drinks. It's a wonder their teeth haven't rotted out. Did you know that - "

A beep marked the end of his time.

"There goes my three minutes," Joe said, tossing his hands in the air. "Remember, folks. All you're worth is three minutes of the school board's time."

Waiting his turn to speak, Walter crinkled a pair of notebook pages with ragged edges. Audience members eyeballed Walter in his pinstripe suit. Week after week, Walter copied the cadence of Martin Luther King and the reassuring tone of a parent. With the Oxioids in full effect, he slurred a bit when speaking.

Good evening, ladies and gentlemen. Lakehaven schools are some of the most diverse schools in the state. As a black father, I commend the school district for embracing students of all ethnicities. You are a breath of fresh air. I grew up as the only black student in an all-white school district. I know what it means to struggle.

I am here tonight because of the children. Bless their little hearts, but they can't tell you what they need from education, much less what they want from education.

The children can't tell you, so I will. Too many teachers only teach children how to pass state tests. This method is like junk food education, subduing the thirst to learn instead of quenching it.

Self-discipline and self-sufficiency are the cornerstones of success. Rather than teaching children to rely on others, let's teach these kids to rely on themselves. Show them how to stand up for the challenge. They will fail from time to time, but do they get back up and try again? If the answer is yes, then we are succeeding.

Rather than teach students to pass a state test, the schools should teach kids how to test themselves.

Let's get busy. Thank you for your time.

Joe and one guy in a wheelchair clapped from the back of the nearly empty room.

Walter crumpled his speech, tossed it into the garbage can and walked out the door. Joe followed behind, digging a pipe and tobacco pouch from his coat pocket, eager to dispense what he knew about the art of persuasion.

"Three more rules of writing: write the way you talk, write what you know and mean what you write," Joe said, blowing a smoke cloud as they drove out of the parking lot. "You only get one shot to make your point with the reader. And remember, reading is an individual experience. Thousands of people may read your column, you see, but they're not all crowded around one copy of the newspaper."

--

The rule for contributing columnists to The Searchlight was that the topic had to be about Lakehaven. County and state topics were welcome as long as there was a tie to Lakehaven. The newspaper could not restrain Walter, mostly because he was black and pulled the race card. No topic was off-base.

Walter wrote his own headlines, ranging from "Thank God, Black History Month is over" to "The education of a black father." If the editor demanded a Lakehaven connection, Walter simply added some non-sequiter sentence, then moved on to what he wanted to talk about, whether it was education, race, his daughter, or all three. The column was a sales pitch, honed to perfection. He could sell sunglasses to a blind man, including Ernest, the editor who masqueraded as a disgruntled typist. But that's what made the column sing.

It was time to fine-tune Walter's latest entry on the fly. He orated with a narcotic buzz as the fully caffeinated Ernest typed. Ernest thought this method was much easier than slogging through Walter's chicken-scratch cursive on ragged-edged notebook paper.

> Message for a black child
> By Walter Wadsworth, Searchlight columnist
>
> Like you, I was different than all the other children. I was the only black kid at an all-white school.
>
> I ate lunch alone in an empty classroom while the rest of the children laughed in the cafeteria. No one drank after me at the water fountain. I waited at the end of the line while the white kids quenched their thirst. There was no separate water fountain for black kids at this school, although I admit it: I wished there was.
>
> The children, parents and even the teachers said my hair was nappy. They mocked my secondhand clothing. They pointed at my beat-up shoes and unflattering physical features. One boy asked if he could borrow a bicycle pump for my lips. Even after all these years, I remember his remark whenever I look in the mirror.
>
> One day, the lights were turned off for my class to watch a film.
>
> "It's so dark in here. I can't see you, Walter. Can you please smile?" The class roared with laughter at the teacher's cruel joke. I desperately wanted to fit in with the other kids. I admit it: I wished I were white.
>
> I knew there was a better path that awaited me. I refused to let those kids stand in the way.
>
> I became the first in my family to earn a college degree, and I will do everything in my power to ensure that

my daughter has even more opportunities.

I am a believer in redemption. I have seen the promised land. I live as though my worst fears will never come true. I look for a light from above to guide me home.

Today's children embody Martin Luther King's dream. I have seen it in my daughter's classroom in Lakehaven. I watch as she lets go of my hand and plays with blacks, whites and Asians.

Dr. King would be proud to see his legacy endure, for in today's world, there is no room for hatred.

In today's world, my daughter is one step closer to being judged not by the color of her skin, but by the content of her character.

In a perfect world, we could save all the children from harm and suffering. In the real world, the struggle will outlive us all.

I have seen the best that humanity has to offer, and I want to shine a light for my daughter to follow. I will choose the mountaintop of hope, rather than the valley of despair. I will make the journey for our children.

To the parents, I say: If we don't show the next generation how to reach the mountaintop, who will?

To the children, I say: I believe in you.

Walter's readers

Walter seduced readers into a frenzy with his Searchlight columns. As a writer, his growth and reputation soared.

"When are you going to run for office?" said some letters.

"Give 'em hell and keep telling it like it is," said others.

"Thank you for standing up for what you believe."

"Why do you keep printing Walter Wadsworth's liberal touchy-feely drivel? He makes me gag."

"Thank you for running Walter Wadsworth's column. It's the first thing I read."

"There you go again, showing me the light."

"There you go again, printing rubbish by another empty-headed conservative blowhard. What does Walter Wadsworth know about abortion rights? If men could have babies, abortion clinics would be on every corner. I am insulted that The Searchlight would endorse such an opinion. Please cancel my subscription to this worthless rag."

"What a thought-provoking article, Walter. I clipped it and mailed it to my sister in Texas. These tree-hugging liberals ought to be ashamed. Have they no morals?"

"I did not receive my Searchlight this morning. I need my weekly dose of Walter Wadsworth."

"We may not always agree, but I respect your opinion."

It was through the column that Walter connected with a Seattle Seahawks executive.

"Walter, I admire your courage in standing up for what you believe," the executive wrote Walter, in response to a column titled "I'm not on the black side, just the right side."

The executive invited Walter to the hottest pro football game of the season.

"The world needs more honest voices like yours," the executive wrote to Walter. "Included with this letter are four tickets to the club suite. You are welcome to bring your family and enjoy yourselves when the Seahawks take on the San Francisco 49ers. Thank you again for saying what so many people can't or won't say out loud. I look forward to shaking your hand."

Walter sold the tickets for pills and cash. He watched the Seahawks game from a rabbit-eared TV at the Shady Acres Motel. On the nightstand was an orange prescription bottle next to a box of Magnums, the name stamped in gold letters on the package.

--

After the publication of "Message for a black child," six readers reached out to Walter, and one invited him to coffee at a cafe near Mount Rainier Elementary.

Walter was greeted by Bud McKenzie, a seventy-something white and bald retiree with smoke-stained fingernails that gripped the ball end of a wooden cane. He motioned for the waitress to bring Walter a cup of coffee.

"I read your column religiously," he told Walter as they sat down. "It is a pleasure to finally meet you in person."

"Well it is a pleasure to meet you," Walter said. "I'm glad you enjoy the column. If I can reach just one reader, then it's all worthwhile."

"I imagine you reach more than one reader," Bud said, pausing to sip his coffee. "How long have you been a writer?"

"I've always been a writer. I just didn't know it until later in life," Walter said, smiling.

"As far as your views on education, I agree with you one-hundred percent," he said. "I'm glad somebody has the courage to tell it like it is."

"I do it for the children, especially my daughter," Walter said. "Did your children go to Lakehaven schools?"

"Yes, all four of them," he said. "That was a long time ago, back when Lakehaven schools were actually decent. Back before all the riff-raff started moving here."

"I know what you mean."

"Now they have all these state tests and federal mandates and teachers who are afraid to hurt kids' feelings if they don't get an A."

"Times have changed."

"I don't mean to get on my soapbox, but these poor test scores are unacceptable," Bud said. "So is the school district's lack of competency in educating all the ethnic minorities, if you know what I mean."

"True," Walter said.

"That's why your column is such a breath of fresh air. You articulate these things better than I ever could," Bud said. "You can't fix education by throwing money at it. You need to transform the attitude and mindset that screwed it up in the first place."

"Lakehaven schools have a tendency to get that reaction."

Almost an hour had passed since the conversation shifted to Bud McKenzie's war stories. Walter made an excuse to go to the restroom, where he popped a pill for the road.

"It's been a pleasure meeting you," Walter said upon returning to the table. "I have an appointment at The Search-light in ten minutes, and I need to catch the bus. It's times like these when a car would be handy."

"Let me give you a ride," Bud said, standing up and reaching for his cane. "I'm heading that direction anyway."

They climbed into Bud's royal blue Lincoln Town Car with white leather interior and handicapped license plates. A week later, Walter invited Bud to coffee at the same place and borrowed sixty dollars. Although Bud eventually sought repayment, they never saw each other again.

"Is Walter Wadsworth available?" Bud asked The Searchlight receptionist on the phone. "He writes a weekly column for the paper."

"Trust me, I know who Walter is," the receptionist said. "He's actually not an employee here. He's an independent contractor."

"He's a what?" Bud asked.

"An independent contractor. He gets paid by the column," she said. "If you didn't know any better, you'd think he lived here."

"Does he have a phone number where I can reach him?"

"Let me check," she said, leafing through her Rolodex, landing on Walter Wadsworth's card, which showed a phone number written in black pen.

"Thank you, ma'am," Bud said. He hung up the phone with the receptionist and dialed the number. The phone rang four times before the voicemail greeting took over.

"Hello," said the voicemail greeting. "You've reached Joe Lippy. I'm not in right now, so leave your name and number after the beep, and I'll get back to you as soon as I can."

Walter's new pals

The Searchlight printed a Latino columnist every Saturday. That writer, Alberto Morales, worked his way up in the food industry, from dishwasher to executive chef, before finally opening his own restaurant, Morales Mexican Grill.

Alberto called his weekly column The Whole Enchilada.

"Why do you keep running this guy?" Walter asked, looking at Alberto's column in the paper. "All he talks about is Mexican food."

"Everybody loves Alberto," Ernest said. "Plus I love the name of his column."

"The Whole Enchilada? You should call it Spic and Span."

"Hey man, don't insult Alberto," Ernest said, reaching for his coffee mug. "He's a great guy. Donates a lot of time and food. He recently won a humanitarian award for volunteering at a soup kitchen in Seattle."

"He needs to spice up his column, that's all I'm saying. He should write about the Latino teen pregnancy rate in Lakehaven schools. That's worth reading about."

Walter leaned back and propped his feet on Ernest's desk as he thumbed through the paper.

"What's this?" Walter said, sitting forward, holding the open paper at attention, reading the headline: "Sex offender caught with camera at Lakehaven Children's Museum." A mug shot showed a cross-eyed creep in his mid-thirties, a ring of stringy hair horseshoeing his bare scalp. According to the report, the man had hidden two cameras in the girls bathroom, including one inside the toilet bowl.

"I am disgusted," Walter said. "My daughter and I go to the children's museum."

"The article said the man was hired a month ago. Have you and Lilly visited in that time?"

"No, it's been a while," Walter said, relieved but tense. "Lilly loves that place. Every kid in Lakehaven loves that place."

"Don't worry, they'll take care of him in prison. He'll be some big black guy's bitch."

"Damn right. If I ever see that piece of shit on the streets, I'll kick his ass."

Walter finished reading the article.

"The story says his last known address was a homeless shelter in Seattle. Wonder if it's the same place where The Whole Enchilada helps out."

"Alberto said he works at the shelter off MLK Drive."

"So he works with the perverts, huh?" Walter sneered. "You know what they say. Birds of a feather flock together."

Ernest slammed his palm on the desk, shaking coffee out of the mug.

"You can think what you want about Alberto, but when you're in this office, I don't want to hear it. Got it?"

Walter folded the paper and tucked it under an arm as he stood. "OK."

"All right then. Let's tackle your column on Wednesday."

"Sounds good. Listen, Ernest, when you get a minute, could you give me a lift to a friend's house? I can wait in the lobby until you're ready."

Ernest sighed, tapped a pen for a few beats, stood up and

turned off the light as he followed Walter out of the office.

--

There wasn't a cloud in the pure blue sky. Sweat beaded on Walter's face as he carried his coat over his shoulder. The sunshine felt like a hug. So did the pills that he swallowed while waiting for a ride in Ernest's Jeep.

The clicks and bells of a mechanical typewriter grew louder as Walter approached the window of Joe Lippy's bedroom cave. With his nose an inch from the window screen, Walter watched Joe's two pointed index fingers tap the keys like piston hammers.

When the typing paused, Walter knocked.

"Ahhh!" Joe said, startled off-balance. "Damn it, just knock at the front door."

That afternoon, tucked in the cave with the wine on autopilot, Joe waxed poetic.

"Lazy teachers lead to lazy students, you see," Joe said, lighting his pipe and blowing a nimbus cloud of smoke all over the desk and Walter. "If I were on the school board, I'd scrap all this watered down, Mickey Mouse bullshit they teach in Lakehaven schools."

Joe moved the wine bottle and cleared space on a table in his cave. He put two encyclopedias side by side. The encyclopedia on the left was open at the entry for cilia.

"Here's something the kids aren't learning about in Lakehaven," Joe said, pointing with a crooked finger at the page. "Look at this photo of bacteria, as seen by an electron microscope. The tiny hairs, or cilia, resemble grasses and shrubs, but in the case of bacteria, the cilia act as a motor."

"Uh huh," said Walter, glassy eyed as the drugs took effect.

"People need to compare the largest with the smallest, you see," Joe said, wobbling atop the stool by the window, hunched over the encyclopedia. "The image of a cluster of hairs under an electron microscope, you see, looks similar in texture to a desert landscape."

"Joe, I don't follow," said Walter, fighting droopy eyelids.

"Everything is relative. Everything has an equal and opposite reaction. The cilia that covers the bacteria are like the hairs on our own heads and bodies, but only a smaller version, you see."

Another encyclopedia was open in the middle of the L volume. The entry was for the term "life." A photo on one-fourth of the page showed a landscape from the Sonoran Desert in Arizona, where Saguaro cactuses dotted the terrain like erect soldiers.

"The desert landscape and the electron microscope photos both show landscapes, just on a different scale," Joe said. "If humans were the size of flies, for example, consider how much bigger the Earth would appear. And in the scheme of the universe, the Earth is a mere cell itself, you see. Like a speck of sand on a beach."

"Uh huh," said Walter.

"The Earth could be one cell inside a whole giant living being made of cells," Joe said. "Earth must surely be like one cell within a giant body. Does that make sense?"

"Uh huh."

"Well they need to teach this shit in Lakehaven schools," Joe said, swigging from a bottle of merlot.

Walter was stoned.

"Every aspect of life," Joe said, pausing to hiccup, "is related somehow, and in some way."

"Listen," Walter said. "I'm seeing Lilly this weekend and hoped you could -"

"Did I ever show you my orange?"

Joe once let an orange rot on a stool next to his piano. Now the fruit was gray, hard and hollow.

"The orange represents the Earth. I set out to see if mold would destroy the orange's resources the same way people devour the Earth's resources," Joe said. "The peculiar thing with this orange, you see, is that I started the experiment almost a year ago. The orange is petrified, as you can see here."

Joe handed the hardened orange to Walter.

"The orange was once a fleshy fruit, like a uterus for the tree, you see," Joe said. "Like a uterus, a fruit's function ripens to a peak. Then it starts to decline."

Joe shifted from foot to foot, listening to his own voice.

"Sometimes," Joe continued, "a piece of fruit decomposes. Mold and maggots devour it, you see."

Walter nodded.

"Humans devour the Earth's nutrients like mold devours an orange. The Earth is like a big fertile uterus, like an orange, you see," Joe said. "Humanity has tapped the Earth's vital fluids, such as oil and natural gas and so on."

Walter was on the brink of vertigo.

"And like the bacteria that give off gas and toxins," Joe continued, "humans give off gas and toxins. When bacteria give off gas and toxins within our bodies, we get sick. When humans give off gas and toxins, we make the Earth sick."

Walter momentarily snapped out of his Oxioid stupor. "What the hell are you talking about?" he asked.

"Humans give the Earth a fever," Joe said. "That's the only idea Al Gore ever said that made sense."

Joe pulled a three-inch thick binder from a shelf and leafed through the middle pages. He stopped on a drawing of the Earth spinning like a top.

"Here's the real answer to global warming," Joe said. "The Earth spins on its axis as it revolves around the sun. When a top is spinning, it reaches a point where it wobbles, you see, and spins beyond its original parameters."

Joe happened to have one of the classic children's toys. He

44

spun the top on a patch of open floor. The two men watched in silence.

"There it is," Joe said at the moment the spin died down. "You see, the top takes a few turns to straighten back up. That's what the Earth is doing. We are temporarily wobbling an extra hundred million miles or so closer to the sun, just as we wobbled away from the sun to create the Ice Age."

"Joe," Walter said, "You lost me a long time ago."

The smile faded from Joe's face. He reached for a new wine bottle on the desk.

"Well they thought Galileo was crazy for suggesting the Earth revolved around the sun," Joe said. "My point is that these damn schools need to teach kids how to think against the grain."

Walter stood up to leave.

"I'm seeing Lilly this weekend. Spot me fifty bucks?"

"OK."

"I need another favor tonight," said Walter, putting a hand on Joe's shoulder. "I need to borrow your car again."

Room at the inn

Joe Lippy and his middle-aged girlfriend lived together. More accurately, Joe lived in his girlfriend's middle-class house.

All of his belongings, books mostly, packed an entire bedroom, with a window on the ground floor and a shaded trunk view of a coastal redwood that swallowed the front yard. Joe respected that tree because of how fast it grew in the decades since he planted it.

In his pajamas, Joe piddled and played alone in a corner of the room. He sat at his computer, in front of a screened window, shadowed by the mighty redwood. He was writing a letter to The Searchlight in response to an editorial on gun control when Walter popped up at the window like a jack in the box.

"Yow! Goddamn it Walter, just go to the front door and knock," Joe said, catching his breath. "For Christ's sake, all my neighbors can see is a black man peeping in my window."

"Listen, I need my shoes. They're in your car," Walter said. "The doors are locked."

Joe wiped his runny nose on a pajama sleeve and puffed his pipe. With smoke leaking out his mouth and nose, he slid off a padded stool and jarred a pair of empty wine bottles. He walked out the door, not acknowledging Walter, eyes fixed on the Rabbit as he pulled the car keys from a pocket on his terry cloth robe. He unlocked the passenger-side door of the Rabbit and shuffled back indoors. If Walter spoke in those moments, Joe wasn't listening. The day was almost done, the setting sun felt good through the window, and he wasn't in the mood for Walter's charity spiel. Give anything to Walter once, whether it was money or labor, and he pushed for more.

Joe tired from Walter's pressure, as did most people - that is, the people who dealt with Walter day to day, like a habit. A few times, Joe loaned Walter money. A few times, Walter made Joe feel important. They both won with this setup.

That evening, a new manager at the Shady Acres Motel denied Walter a room because he lacked the cash, and his charm fell flat. He and his shiny white sneakers splashed back toward Joe's neighborhood, three miles away.

Inside the comfort of his furnished living room, Joe sipped wine and watched "The Tonight Show." Meanwhile, Walter walked the suburban sidewalks, his clothes and white baseball cap soaked by the rain. A garment bag hung over his shoulder, protecting his pinstripe suit from the elements. He wore a gray wool sweater and blue jeans, cloaked in a black trench coat.

Inside Walter's satchel was a pen, a spiral notebook and a hardback edition of "The Power of Positive Thinking."

As if he lived in the neighborhood all his life, Walter strolled up to the Rabbit in Joe's driveway. The window to Joe's room by the front door was dark. So was the yard and driveway. The only light on this part of the street was a street light, standing tall a few yards down, generating enough light to read the house numbers that were painted on the curb.

The car's dented door squawked open. Walter shoved his bags into the back seat and climbed into the reclined passenger seat. He pulled the edge of the oil-stained blanket close to his chin and covered his face with the white hat, blocking the street light's incandescent glare.

He closed his eyes and fell asleep.

--

Three days later, the bedside telephone's frantic midnight ringing awakened Joe from a saucy dream in which he was banging Diane Sawyer as she delivered a newscast about guns.

"Joe, the car won't start. Please, my friend, can you come over and look at it?"

"Damn it, Walter, what are you talking about?" Joe rubbed his eyes and looked at the clock. "I drove that car every day for the past eight years."

"Come on, Joe, you know I'd do anything for you," Walter said. "The car won't start, and it's cold outside. I'm at the shopping center on Foster Street near Sixth Avenue."

"Fine," Joe said after a moment of silence. "Give me fifteen minutes."

"Thank you my friend."

"I'm not loaning you any money."

"Understood."

Joe arrived to find Walter loitering by the pay phone, with one foot on the white Rabbit's front bumper. Joe had given the car to Walter, signing over the title and even paying the transfer fee.

Before, they had an agreement that Walter would only sleep in the car between 10 p.m. and 5 a.m.

Joe's girlfriend found out, and the driveway no longer housed Walter's de facto motel room. Walter parked the car at a 24-hour shopping center until Lakehaven Code Enforcement told him to move.

Joe rode up in a rusty pea green Cadillac and squeaked to a stop next to the Rabbit. He stepped out in his robe, striped pajamas and leather boots. He walked up to the Rabbit's open front hood and grimaced.

"Well I'll be damned. This thing really is shot," said Joe, shaking his head in disbelief. "In fact, it looks like it was shot with a .44 Magnum."

Joe refused to pay for a tow truck. Not this time, he thought.

"Walter, why don't you sleep at a shelter? Or camp in the woods or a state park?"

"Come on, Joe. You know black people don't camp. And I ain't going to no shelter. No way."

They shrugged and, with a simultaneous groan, slowly pushed the Rabbit across Foster Street toward a vacant parking lot.

"Damn, my back," Joe said, grunting, knees crackling.

"Keep pushing!"

"Damn it, my knees!"

"Almost there!"

The crawling car gained momentum, cleared the curb and rolled to a rest in the parking lot of an abandoned supermarket across the street.

Joe was hunched with his hands on his knees, catching his breath.

"Walter, be careful," he said, handing him a twenty dollar bill. "Here, take this."

"Thank you, my friend."

A week later, Walter found a note on the windshield to move the car. He called Joe again, and in ebony and ivory comradeship, they pushed the car down a sloped portion of Foster Street to an empty field. The impact between the curb and the wheels sent the front hubcaps flying in opposite directions. Walter borrowed $10 for a meal and ate pills for supper.

A week later, another rain-soaked note graced the car's cracked windshield. This time, Walter did not call Joe.

Walter tried to move the car with one hand on the steering wheel and two feet on the ground. He gave up and left the car at the vacant lot. He caught the late-night bus to Seattle.

Walter's car title was listed under Joe's address.

Joe received a dozen letters about unpaid fees for the car's impoundment, culminating in a final notice that the car would be destroyed if left unclaimed.

Walter was broke. At the junkyard, Lakehaven Auto Wreckers crushed the Rabbit into a cube.

God bless you, Mr. Wadsworth

Losing the car - for both lodging and transportation - wasn't much of a setback for Walter. He still made the rounds to The Searchlight, Joe's house, Mount Rainier Elementary, Shady Acres Motel, bus station and any restaurant or coffee shop where someone else was buying.

One of Walter's favorite hangouts was the Lakehaven Public Library, where his sex connections flourished. He leered at the computer screen like an Ivy League prodigy, engrossed in deep thought, but instead of scanning headlines, he cruised for escorts.

Walter instructed his latest kinky playmate to meet at The Searchlight, where he claimed to work forty hours a week. She had complimented his distinguished column photo that was published every weekend.

Walter barged into Ernest Handsy's office, escorted by a mature redhead who drove them to The Searchlight.

"Pleasure to meet you," the editor said, blushing as the redhead excused herself to the restroom.

"She's a hooker," Walter whispered.

Ernest raised his eyebrows. "Say what?"

"She's a hooker," Walter said, "and tonight, she's going to let me beat the shit out of her."

Walter whipped out a bundle of Polaroids from his satchel. One photo showed the same redhead, on her hands and knees, eating from a dog dish. She wore a black leather bra with metal studs and a spiked dog collar.

"So," said Ernest, face flushed, reaching for his coffee mug. "Any plans for the weekend?"

"I'm going to meet her again on Saturday," Walter said. "Personal business."

"You're one busy man," Ernest said. "And no, I will not give you a ride."

On Saturday, Walter took the bus to the Wishing Well Motel, arriving a half-hour early for his date. The motel office was locked and dark. He waited on a wooden bench that was carved with initials and obscenities.

The weather had taken a sudden turn with a fluke summer day in mid-spring. A sweaty Walter didn't know which one he wanted more: hot sex or an air-conditioned room.

He gulped his last Oxioid and waited for the swimmy feeling to take hold.

"Sir," said a voice from a fence that flanked the motel.

On the other side of that fence were senior assisted condominiums, well taken care of.

"Sir," said a voice from behind the fence. "Sir, can you come here please?"

Walter leaned forward, trying to look through the slits in the wooden fence. He saw an elderly woman, who stood at the kitchen window in her bathrobe.

"Sir," she said from the window. "I think there's a man on my roof. He's trying to get into my home. I think he may be dumping poison into my air vents."

"Ma'am, stay right here," Walter said. "I'll come around to the front door."

When she opened the door, she recognized him.

"Oh my Lord, you write for the Lakehaven Searchlight,"

she said, her eyes wide at this random celebrity encounter. "I read your column every Saturday. Quick, come inside."

Walter figured the lady's wits were dimming a bit, but played along, hoping she would loan him a few bucks for his post-sex bus ride.

"Is the man on your roof right now?" Walter asked, glancing up at the ceiling.

"Shhh! Not so loud. He can hear us," she said, holding her wrinkled index finger to her lips. She poured two cups of tea, then opened a magazine-sized calendar. Each square in the calendar, leading up to that day's date, was filled with micro-size cursive notes written in blue ballpoint pen. The rest of the calendar was blank.

"Ma'am, I didn't see anyone on your roof when I walked over," Walter said. He knew her mind was made up. He knew she was lonely. "Do you have a ladder?"

They walked to her storage shed across the manicured golf course quality lawn, and returned to the condo with a 12-foot aluminum ladder.

Walter leaned the ladder against the roof. The metal was already hot from the direct sun on a cloud-free day.

When reaching the flat roof, Walter saw a few pine cones and a handful of shingles in a pile next to the brick chimney. He was hot and sweaty and late to his rendezvous.

"Ma'am," he said. "I am pleased to report that the only man on your roof is me."

"Are you sure?" she said.

"Positive," he said, stepping down.

She embraced Walter. "Thank you so much."

"It's no trouble at all, ma'am," Walter laughed. "By the way, I was hoping you might help. I lost my wallet and - "

"God bless you, Mr. Wadsworth," she said, unaware she was interrupting. "You're just as handsome in person as you are in the newspaper."

"Thank you, ma'am," he said, tipping his white baseball hat. "Good day to you."

Walter speed-walked around the corner to the motel and saw his date pacing outside the room on the far side of the complex, the closest room to the fence separating the motel from the condo.

"How did you get so hot and sweaty?" she asked.

"I don't let my right hand know what my left hand is doing," said Walter, bringing his hands to hers.

"Daddy, which hand are you going to spank me with?" she asked, batting her eyelashes. "I've been a bad girl."

With the devil in their eyes, Walter squeezed her hands like a stern Daddy should.

H.N.I.C.

Christian Castle's idle hands do the devil's work
By Walter Wadsworth, Searchlight columnist

The Christian Castle's recent behavior would make
Jesus cry.

Pastor Levi Cooke is not the same guy we knew from
his pro football career. His church's backlighted billboard
spells out his stances on abortion, gay marriage, gun
control, the governor, the Seahawks, global warming, you
name it. The sign attempts to be cute, but fails like an ugly
duckling. This morning, the sign said: "If man evolved
from monkeys, why are there still monkeys?"

I don't know if Jesus was a conservative or a liberal,
and I don't care whether he believed in evolution or
creationism. Jesus wanted the best for humanity. He built
a moral compass and followed his conscience. He led a
revolution by setting an example for love.

If Jesus were pastor of Christian Castle, Jesus would
be too busy for politics and too bright for ignorant one-
liners. He would have used the church's billboard to
enlighten instead of inflame.

Besides the lack of logic, the church sign shows no

love for the enemy of its message. Last I heard, we are supposed to love our enemies and even turn the other cheek. That billboard reinforces the pastor's beliefs and irritates those who disagree. Well guess what, pastor? The billboard irritates people who agree with you, too.

The time devoted toward that billboard is time lost in strengthening education. By wasting time on a provocative billboard, the pastor drains himself of time to act.

The billboard may get a reaction out of passing drivers, but they forget it moments later. What's missing is a call to action. What's missing is the inspiration to get our hands dirty in the trenches. If the pastor and the church channeled their energies toward tutoring children of immigrant families, for example, they could make an impression that lasts. The church can substitute billboard rants with a notice for after-school enrichment courses.

If today's youth are the fruit we bear for tomorrow, then let's help them be fruitful.

When serving the children, either you're on the school bus, or you're not. I will ride the bus until my dying day. The fight never ends. I may not live to see the day when every school in Lakehaven and America has the necessary resources to serve our children.

But I will go down fighting.

When it comes to serving the schools, let's ask ourselves: is the Christian Castle on the bus?

Instead of focusing on politics, the church and Pastor Cooke should ask what Jesus would do for Lakehaven's children and the community they call home.

--

Coincidentally, the largest sum Walter ever hustled was ten-thousand dollars, courtesy of the Christian Castle.

Walter's latest column poked at Pastor Levi Cooke, a former Seattle Seahawks linebacker who built a megachurch in Lakehaven. Cooke was tall, black, muscular, charismatic and handsome. Lakehaven political insiders speculated that the outspoken Cooke could run for the state Legislature and win.

A church secretary contacted Walter, through The Searchlight, to set up a meeting to discuss the column.

On the morning of their meeting, Walter stepped off the bus and walked two blocks to the Christian Castle, which looked less like a church and more like a non-descript office building. The church had struggled to open because of zoning and permits. Roads were built and traffic lights were installed to accommodate thousands of congregants.

Walter was greeted by Levi Cooke at the door.

"Pastor Cooke, it's a pleasure," he said, locked in a royal handshake.

"Nice to meet the man behind the column," said Cooke, whose gold watch sparkled. "Would you like some coffee?"

Their footsteps echoed in the spacious Pine Sol-scented entryway en route to the cafe. The place was quiet at eight o'clock on a Monday morning. The Christian Castle lacked any sign of Christianity. There were no crucifixes or pictures of Jesus. Posters on the walls showed Cooke dressed in a shiny suit with an arm around his wife, Monique, advertising a worship camp.

Walter and Cooke sat down at a table for two in the corner. A barista brought two hot mugs of dark roasted java.

"I love your column, Walter. I read it every Saturday."

"Thank you, pastor."

"I even liked the column where you teased me about the billboard," Cooke said with a chuckle. "It motivated me to reflect on my actions."

"Pastor, you're a good man who could do great things for Lakehaven," said Walter, fidgeting with his mug. "You should run for the Legislature. I bet you'd win."

"Thank you, I'm flattered," Cooke said. "And on that note, please give me some warning before you smack me around in The Searchlight."

They laughed and sipped more coffee.

"Walter, another reason I asked to meet with you is because you seem connected with the schools," Cooke said. "You mentioned in one column - the title escapes me at the moment, but you talked about teachers who spend their own money on classroom supplies."

"Yes," Walter said. "It's quite common in Lakehaven schools."

"Is there a particular school that needs help more than the others?"

"Mount Rainier Elementary School," Walter said with wide eyes. "They're still using overhead projectors from the 1960s. They need digital projectors."

"What's different about the digital projectors?"

"They stream video and live broadcasts. Teachers can plug them into computers," Walter said. "Studies show that kids score higher on tests because they're more engaged with the curriculum. I could go on and on."

"Interesting," Cooke said. "How did you learn about this?"

"I volunteer at Mount Rainier Elementary," he said. "My daughter goes there. Her classroom is trying to raise money to buy a projector just for her class. In reality, all the classrooms need one."

"Maybe the Christian Castle can bless these students with a donation before summer break," Cooke said.

"Pastor, these kids deserve all the blessings they can get," Walter said. "Every little bit helps."

"How much is one projector?"

"About eight-hundred dollars."

"How much do you need," Cooke said, "to get one in

every classroom?"

--

Two hours later, Walter barged into Ernest Handsy's office.

"I don't have time to chat," Ernest said, taking off his glasses. "I'm on deadline right now."

"I'll only take a moment of your time."

Ernest nodded and swiveled his chair.

"I just had coffee with Levi Cooke."

"I need to get in touch with him," Ernest said. "Rumor has it that he plans to run for the Legislature this year."

"That I don't know," Walter said. "I do know that he is donating ten-thousand dollars to buy digital projectors for every classroom at Mount Rainier Elementary."

"I knew it! I'll bet you dollars to doughnuts that his name will be on the November ballot."

"You may be right," Walter said. "Listen, this is a big deal. I need you to write a story and take a photo for the front page when we present the check to the superintendent."

"You know how to get whatever you want from people," Ernest said. "You have the gift."

"That's why they call me the H.N.I.C.," he said. "Head Nigger In Charge."

The next afternoon, the editor and Walter drove to meet Levi Cooke at Superintendent Harvey Oakes's office. On the way, they made a pit stop at Lane's Pharmacy. Walter scored a new prescription and ate two pills right away.

The school's longtime principal joined the group. Ernest's photo showed four respectable members of society. Walter's eyes were glazed.

As the meeting concluded, Walter motioned to the editor that he needed to talk with the superintendent in private.

Through a thin window in the closed office door, Ernest

saw the men laughing. He did not see the superintendent give Walter cash.

After the meeting, Ernest dropped off Walter at the bus station. Walter grinned as he ducked out the door.

"Nice work, Walter."

"Head nigger in charge," he said, his smile reflecting the afternoon sun. "Head nigger in charge."

That night, a fellow addict at the Lakehaven bus station punched an intoxicated Walter in the mouth and knocked out three front teeth.

A nose for friends

Walter kept his three missing front teeth in the satchel.

The addict who split Walter's lip and socked out those top-row incisors had only wanted a fast exit with free pills. The next morning, after the all-night bus ride, Walter took a warm shower at Joe's house, scored an appointment with Joe's dentist, and later rode the bus to the Glitter Ballet Studio in downtown Lakehaven.

That night was Lilly's ballet recital. Walter had promised to attend, so he turned down an appointment to get his teeth fixed. The dentist's next available opening was in three weeks.

"I can live a few more weeks without my front teeth," said Walter, upper lip still swollen, head swimming in opiates. He remembered how his father was a drill sergeant when it came to dental care, which led to Walter's lifelong habit of brushing and flossing every morning. This childhood memory of his father filled the grown-up Walter with shame.

Lilly had begun ballet lessons shortly after her parents divorced. Her mother wanted to find a positive outlet for her daughter's divorce-induced stress. Lilly didn't know the story about Walter's dalliances that destroyed the family. All she knew was that her mother hated her father, and that her father lived somewhere else.

Moments after he arrived at the ballet studio, Walter's ex-wife went apeshit when he said hello.

"Leave me alone!" Rose shouted in the lobby. "If you want to be useful in your daughter's life, then pay child support."

"Listen, Rose, calm down," slurred Walter, who had no declared wages for the courts to garnish. "We don't want to embarrass Lilly."

"Maybe she ought to hear this," Rose said. "She ought to know that her father is a bum."

"Rose, I can explain," he said. "The court needs to - "

"Get the hell out of here," she said. "By the way, what happened to your teeth? Someone give you the ass-whipping you deserve?"

"Listen, bitch," he said, eyebrows furled. "Nobody stops me from seeing my daughter."

Walter headed toward the auditorium where the dancers were warming up. Rose stood in front to block him. He grabbed Rose by her blouse and shoved her against the wall, smacking her head on the bricks.

"Police!" Rose screamed. "Call the police!"

The performers stopped their twirling to gawk at the scene through the open auditorium doors. Walter and Lilly made eye contact. She waved and smiled, and he waved back. Walter's hand covered his mouth when smiling. Lilly's pink ballet costume clung to her sweaty belly, framed by a tutu.

"Call the police!" Rose yelled.

Walter spun around and stumbled out of the studio. Someone called the cops. The grade-school girls in pink tutus, Lilly included, were spared the sight of two officers handcuffing Walter and stuffing him into a police cruiser with red and blue flashing lights. When asking later about her father's whereabouts, Lilly was told he left without explanation.

At the Lakehaven police station, Walter was allowed to make one phone call.

"Joe, I'm in jail. It's a long story."

"Jesus Christ, Walter - what the hell happened this time? I bet you're wasted on those pills."

"Let's worry about that later."

"Did you call a bail bondsman?"

"Joe, please."

"Fine," Joe said. "I'll get there when I get there. You owe me."

--

Walter got a ride to the check-cashing store before Joe swerved him over to Mount Rainier Elementary, minutes before the afternoon bell. Out of the car stepped the most colorful bum in Lakehaven history with a wad of cash from state disability benefits. The money covered motels and hookers. He peddled pills to supplement the rest. Any cash leftover, he spent on Lilly.

He waited on a park bench in the school's shaded courtyard as the kids were dismissed. Lilly skipped toward her father, with a lollipop like a golf ball in her cheek.

"Daddy!" Lilly shrieked, stopping in her steps, pulling the red candy out of her mouth. "What happened to your teeth? Did you get in a fight?"

Walter said he got hit in the mouth with a baseball while umpiring a Little League game. It was true that he began earning cash as a Little League ump that spring.

"Enough about me," he said, holding a palm in front of his mouth. "How did you do on that math test?"

"Pretty good, I think," she said. They walked toward the coffee shop. "Thank you for working with me on my multiplication tables. The teacher said I'm getting better."

"I'm so proud of you," Walter said. "Keep it up, sweetheart, and you can be anything you want when you grow up."

"You know what I want to be when I grow up?"

"What?"

"A writer," Lilly said, crunching the last of the lollipop. "Just like you."

"Aw baby girl, you make your old man proud. I had no idea you were interested in writing."

"I started keeping a diary. Sometimes I write poems, but they're not as good as your articles."

"Poems? I'd love to read your poems."

"Really?" she asked, and he nodded. "How do I know if my poems are any good?"

"Baby girl," he said, touching her shoulder. "If you write with love, you'll never be wrong."

She giggled and searched her backpack. She reached behind the teddy bear and pulled out a sheet of lined paper with ragged edges, ripped from a spiral notebook and folded in half. "Here you go. It's called a limerick."

"Did you write this today?"

She nodded. Walter recited the poem out loud.

A Nose For Friends
By Lilly Wadsworth

An odd little gal from the sticks
would only befriend fellow hicks
she said, I suppose,
all hicks like my nose,
'cause it's my nose that everyone picks.

Walter burst into laughter, toothless mouth wide open.

"Do you like it?" she asked. Tears streamed down Walter's laughing face. Other customers in the coffee shop stared. Walter and Lilly laughed and wobbled on padded chairs at a corner table.

"This is amazing," Walter said, wiping his eyes with a sleeve. "I'm not just saying that because you're my daughter. People work their whole lives to write something this good. I'm proud of you."

She batted her eyelashes. "Thank you, Daddy."

Lilly sipped a caramel latte through two skinny straws. Walter drank black coffee in a plain white mug. Lilly liked that her father listened and nodded his head. She recapped her school day. He smiled without covering his toothless grin.

What's a con artist?

In full stride along Lakehaven's cracked sidewalks, Walter approached The Searchlight for another ride to his daughter's house, this time from Ernest.

Even with the rainy wind needling his face, Walter burned off aggression and frustration with every step. Earlier that day, he saw an article about a preschool girl who was hospitalized by her abusive father. According to the report, the man admitted to detectives that he hit the girl with fifty percent of his strength.

"Let me hit that son-of-a-bitch with one-hundred percent of my strength," Walter said out loud, breathing heavy as the traffic hummed past.

Only once did Walter punish his daughter with a spanking, he recalled. Lilly's toddler years were some of the best of his life. Walter craved that baby smell and loved to watch Lilly, in her first years of walking, march through the house in a diaper, her dainty bare feet slapping the linoleum. She loved microwave popcorn, which was a bonus because it was all Walter could cook. She was four years old at the time of the spanking, a precocious preschooler with a defiant streak. On that day, her listening ears, as Walter called them, were broken. She walked on the furniture in her sandals, leaving wood chips and streaks of dirt in her wake. Walter had warned her of the consequences.

"Lilly, you need to turn on your listening ears. This is the third time in the past five minutes that I've asked you to stop climbing on the furniture," Walter said. "If I have to tell you one more time, I'm going to spank you."

Sure enough, a few minutes later, she stomped along the three-cushioned leather couch and jumped the gap to the matching recliner.

Walter turned off the television, cutting off Elmo in mid-sentence. Without saying a word, he grasped Lilly's little wrist and led her into the den. It was the calm before the storm, so to speak. Walter's mouth was dry. He didn't want to hurt her, but didn't want to make empty threats. He had threatened to spank her a few times before, and the threat was usually good enough.

Walter sat down on the love seat and hoisted Lilly across his lap. She giggled.

He breathed slow and deep. He closed his eyes. Guilt and shame flushed his face.

Too soft of a slap would be useless. Too hard of a slap would be abuse. Lilly laid across his lap, pink sweat pants and princess undies pulled down to expose her buttocks. She giggled again. He pressed his left hand between her shoulder blades. Lilly was quiet with curiosity. He raised his right hand toward the stucco ceiling, palm facing out, and with all the re-straint he could muster, Walter cracked his hand like a whip. He delivered two quick stinging spanks - slap! slap!

After three seconds of silence, Lilly cried. It was a full-steam ahead cry. There was a red handprint on her bottom that was redder where the edges of his pinky and ring finger struck the skin.

Walter picked her up and hugged her against his shoulder. She cried and hugged him hard. He rubbed her back.

"Daddy loves you," he said, with tears in his eyes. "Daddy loves you."

--

In the post-divorce years, Lilly grew closer to Grandma, who was Rose's mother. Grandma lived in Lakehaven and visited often.

"Oh good grief, my hemorrhoids are on fire," said Grandma, straining into a chair next to Lilly at the kitchen table after a trip to the bathroom. "You know what they say about Mexican food: spicy going in, spicy going out."

Lilly wrinkled her nose and reached for the potato chips.

The family was accustomed to Grandma's loose-lipped confessions of private thoughts. She reminded everyone in her softest, sweetest tone that at this age, she could say whatever the hell she wanted. The more she guzzled coffee, the faster she chatted, like one of those talking dolls with a string that stretched to the moon.

Lilly was waiting for Walter to pick her up for a visit, and mentioned that her father helped with her math homework. In typical freewheeling style, Grandma shifted the conversation toward memory lane.

"When I was a girl," Grandma said, "I went to Catholic school, and if you misbehaved, the nuns spanked you, even at your age."

"Nuns? Did you have teachers when you went to school?"

"The nuns were the teachers, and they had no tolerance for mischief," Grandma said. "Two weeks before graduation, my brother told a nun to go to hell. The school told my brother they'd let him graduate if he apologized, and he refused. He moved to California instead. He fit right in."

"What did he do in California?"

"Sweetheart, he was a con artist."

"What's a con artist?"

"A con artist is someone who swindles other people for personal gain," Grandma said. "My brother was always a crook. When we were kids, he stole everything from baseball cards to the collection plates from church. He wasn't quite right in the head."

"Did you say he was mentally ill?"

"Yes, sweetie, he was a real cuckoo, among other things," Grandma said. "He was also AC-DC."

"He was in a rock band?" Lilly asked. She imagined Angus Young duck-walking across the stage as he played a guitar solo.

"No, dear. AC-DC is a way of saying he had romantic relationships with both women and men."

"Are all con artists an AC-DC?"

"Heavens no, dear. My brother just had strange preferences," Grandma said. "Con artists come in different packages. They gain people's trust, then take advantage of them."

"What do con artists look like?"

"A friend of ours once had a phony roofing contractor who charged almost four-thousand dollars and never fixed a damn thing. Not one shingle."

"Do I know a con artist?"

Grandma had a loose tongue, but made sure not to utter "your father."

"Not that I'm aware of, dear," she said. "Just remember to steer clear of suspicious people. Sometimes a feeling in the back of your head tells you, 'I'm being used.'"

Lilly was intrigued. In her mind, she pictured an artist painting at an easel while picking the pockets of passing strangers.

"I hope I never meet a con artist," Lilly said. "I don't think I would like one."

"They are despicable people," Grandma said. "Never trust

a con artist."

And with that point made, Grandma somehow shifted the conversation to the "dry birth" and subsequent breast-feeding of her first child forty years ago.

"Now your uncle, he was what we called a barracuda baby. He was a biter when he nursed," Grandma said, making a biting motion, her incisors clicking together. "Of course, he had his front teeth long before his first birthday."

Lilly's eyes widened. Rose shuffled into the kitchen with a broom and dustpan.

"Mom, were you a barracuda baby?" Lilly asked. She and Grandma giggled.

"For crying out loud," Rose said. "Don't talk to my daughter about this shit!"

They all laughed. Rose poured a cup of coffee and sat at the kitchen table.

"Lilly, you better get your shoes on," Rose said. "Your father will be here any minute."

"Does he have to wait outside again?"

"Yes."

"Why? What did he do?"

"There are things about your father that I will not discuss with you," Rose said. "Now please, go get your shoes. They're in your room."

Lilly fetched her white canvas sneakers. She heard the women whispering as she left the kitchen, and the whispers diminished as Lilly reached her bedroom. She flipped the light switch. Her eyes found the picture frames that lined the window ledge. One photo was a studio portrait of Rose and Lilly. One photo showed Grandma and Grandpa with sunburned cheeks on a cruise ship in the Caribbean. The third photo showed Lilly and Walter at a school assembly. Last year as a fourth-grader, Lilly earned straight A's on every report card. In the photo, Lilly held a white certificate, and Walter held Lilly in his arms. Their toothy smiles stretched ear to ear.

"I'm so proud of you," Walter had told Lilly right before the photo was made. "You'll always be my princess."

Lilly laced up her shoes and strolled back to the kitchen with a grin. Rose and Grandma's whispering grew more audible with each step toward the kitchen.

"... and he owes two years worth of child support," Rose said. "I'm never going to see a single cent. I can't believe I buy his excuses."

"Your father and I kept our mouths shut," Grandma said. "But we had a feeling Walter was nothing but a con artist."

"Con artist is too nice of a description," Rose said. "Worthless bum is more accurate."

Lilly stood out of view of the kitchen's entrance and listened.

"Honey, for Lilly's sake, you need to let go of your hatred for him. It's only going to drain your well-being," Grandma said. "Remember, he might be a bum, but Lilly is still his daughter, and she loves him dearly."

"As far as I'm concerned," Rose said, "Lilly is the only good thing Walter gave this world."

There was a knock at the door. "Speaking of bums," Grandma said. She and Rose cackled.

"Lilly, hurry up and get your shoes," Rose called out, thinking Lilly was at the other end of the house. "Your father is here."

Lilly stepped into the kitchen a moment after Rose hollered. She kissed her mom and grandmother goodbye, unlocked the deadbolt and opened the oak front door wide enough to slip through.

"How's my girl today?" said Walter, covering that toothless grin with his hand.

"Fine," she said, turning her head, fiddling with her pink barrette.

"You look sad. What's wrong?"

"Nothing."

"My friend Ernest is going to give us a ride to the coffee shop," he said. "You up for a strawberry smoothie ... with whipped cream?"

"Yeah," she said, finally cracking a smile. Walter wrapped his arm around her as they walked to the editor's idling Jeep.

"Daddy," Lilly said. "Are you a con artist?"

"Where did you hear that?"

"Mom and Grandma."

"I see," said Walter, taking a deep breath as they approached the Jeep. "A con artist is a person you can't trust. But you can trust your own father."

"I trust you, Daddy."

"I know you do, baby girl," he said. "I know."

New teeth

Walter told everyone, including his daughter, that a baseball knocked out his teeth.

The excuse was plausible. He umpired a few Little League games in Lakehaven, earning fifty dollars for calling balls and strikes. The kids were good sports, but the parents behaved like beasts. They hollered and swore without mercy. At the most recent game, one father set the bar even lower when he screamed, "Get your head out of your ass," after Walter had called the runner out at home plate.

For Walter, the gig was easy money. He had heard of it from another umpire who happened to like his column. He was paid to watch two teams of 12-year-olds splash in a water-logged baseball field.

In his final umpire job of the summer, Walter met the unruliest of parents: a drunk dad who was pissed that his kid struck out.

With a lip full of Copenhagen, the dad spat as he walked through the gate and onto the field, pointing and swearing like the tattooed Marine that he was. The man wore a white T-shirt with sleeves that hugged his chiseled arms. He was fit and ready to rumble. This was the second time Walter had called out the Marine's son on a third strike.

The military dog tags jangled from the man's neck as he stepped into Walter's personal space. The man pushed his chest against Walter's padded chest protector, shouting inches from his poker face. The man reeked of beer and Marlboros. Walter waited for tempers to cool.

"I respect you and your service to our country," said Walter, holding his protective mask by the strap. "Please, sir, tone down the language in front of these children."

The half-grinning man stared with one eyebrow cocked: "I'll say whatever the hell I want, you toothless pansy."

Walter turned around and walked to the gate across from first base. The crowd and players watched in silence. Walter unlatched the gate on the chain-link fence, opened it wide, and stood silent like a soldier at attention. The loudmouth dad lowered his head for a moment and walked off the field, out the gate and into the gravel parking lot. A crushed can of Rainier beer fell out when he opened the door to his Ford truck and climbed inside. With metal music blaring, his oversized tires kicked up gravel as he spun away, creating a chorus of scattered dings as pebbles pelted nearby vehicles.

The crowd applauded, Walter tipped his white cap, and the game continued. Near the last inning, Walter decided he hated the coach for one of the teams, the Seagulls. Walter clenched his fists and molars as he observed the coach, who belittled his son in front of the other Seagulls. Before the game started, the coach called the boy a sissy and made him run two laps around the parking lot. Later, when the Seagulls were ahead ten to one, the coach's son was called out on strikes. Once in the dugout, the coach jabbed the boy in the forehead with the knuckle of his middle finger, leaving an instant goose egg welt.

Hours after the game, long after the mainstream world had gone to bed, Walter curled up on the all-night bus seat, warmed by vodka and dulled by meds. He couldn't forget about that boy's forehead and humiliated eyes. He concocted a plan. He wanted to pay two addicts to track down the coach and stomp him in the forehead.

Walter finally passed out on the bus. The coach escaped a beating.

--

The bus ride ended one step ahead of sunrise. Walter grabbed his brown leather satchel and thanked the driver as he stepped off the bus.

"I love your column, Mr. Wadsworth," the driver said. "You just keep telling it like it is."

"Thank you, sir," said Walter, covering his smile, ready to patrol his territory like a stray cat. In his satchel was a copy of "The Power of Positive Thinking."

The sunlight framed the evergreens against the jagged Cascades in the distance, highlighted by Mount Rainier's snowy peak. Morning dew coated every blade of grass for miles.

Walter peered at the crosswalk down the block, then crossed at the middle of the road like he always did, his white sneakers at full stride.

His dental appointment was two hours away, and there was time to kill. The first stop was the coffee shop, open at 5 a.m. Walter sank into a red-cushioned booth, with one white sneaker bouncing on the floor. The steaming coffee idled on the table alongside a blank sheet of paper ripped from a spiral notebook. He swallowed two pills and scrawled the title "The Power of Parenthood" in shaky left-handed penmanship.

He examined the title for a moment. With a frustrated sigh, he slapped down the pen on the table, ripped out the page and tossed the wad into the corner trash can.

--

That afternoon, Walter strolled into Ernest Handsy's office without an appointment.

"Knock knock," said Walter, tapping the door frame before walking in and taking a seat.

"I'm really busy right now," Ernest said, turning toward Walter. "Holy shit! You got new teeth!"

His smile resembled two rows of white piano keys. "Damn right I got new teeth," Walter said, flashing those pearly whites. He set his satchel on the floor and plunked down "The Power of Positive Thinking" on the desk.

"Joe Lippy's dentist over on First Avenue set me up with these sparkling, gleaming white new teeth," Walter said, beaming like a talk show host. "How do they look?"

"You look like a million bucks," Ernest said. "By the way, I just got off the phone with another reader who thinks you're full of shit."

"Who?"

"She refused to give her name, but she described you with enough obscenities to make a sailor blush."

"Bitch."

"On the bright side," said Ernest, removing his glasses, "some old lady called an hour later, wanting to thank you for saying in print what she can't say out loud. She reads every column."

"My peeps know what they like," Walter said of his audience, as loyal as any audience the editor had seen. "How many other papers have a black columnist who can write like me?"

It was true. The Lakehaven Searchlight was the only paper in the area with a black columnist, albeit a homeless addict who appealed to white readers of all classes. Walter took pride in busting stereotypes.

"People assume that if you're black, you'll vote for the Democrat or the black candidate. And to the black community, if you do otherwise, you're a traitor," Walter said. "I've been called everything from an Oreo to an Uncle Tom."

"Maybe you're white at heart," Ernest teased.

"Look, the head knows what the heart feels," Walter said. "I had no qualms about telling the brothers at the barbershop why I voted for the white guy in the governor's race."

"But why wouldn't you want to help elect the state's first black governor?" Ernest asked. "It was a chance to make history and show that MLK's dream had come true."

"What the hell have you been smoking?" Walter asked, hands on his hips. "I'm not going to vote for a black man just because I'm black or he's black. In the black community, this governor is what they call a House Negro."

"As a white man, I could never say that," Ernest said.

"This governor actually had the nerve to say conservatives are all a bunch of racists," Walter said, "when it's his liberals who play the race card."

Ernest sat uncomfortably in his caucasian skin and nodded. This was turf that only Walter could touch, at least in this room, where he once again sucked out all the air.

"Democrats say if you don't support the black governor, you must be a racist," Walter said.

"Aw, come on. It's not that cut and dry."

"Now now, Ernest. Someday you'll see the light, once you get out of the liberal media," said Walter, smiling without covering his mouth. "And by the way, fuck you, I got new teeth."

They laughed.

"Listen, Ernest, if I could ask one favor today, I need a ride to the pharmacy," he said. "Whenever you're ready."

They climbed into the editor's Jeep, freshly christened with Walter's body odor and booze breath. The pharmacy was located inside Safeway a few miles away. The pharmacists all knew Walter, as did the cashiers and janitors.

His prescription for painkillers was ready in minutes.

Ernest waited around because Walter needed a ride to the bus station.

"Thank you, my friend," Walter said as they pulled up to the bus station. He handed Ernest a crumpled twenty dollar bill and stepped out of the Jeep. The editor was speechless, his mouth agape.

A scrap of paper

Walter burst through the editor's office door with wide eyes and a scrap of paper.

"Keep this in a safe place," he said, slapping the paper on the desk. "If something happens to me, call this number."

"Don't do anything crazy," Ernest said, motioning to close the door. "What's wrong? Is this something that's going to happen sooner or later?"

"Could be my hepatitis C," Walter said. "Could be my heart. Please do me this favor. If something happens to me, call my brother Harold. He lives in L.A."

The editor assumed Walter was baiting him with an emotional tale to weaken his defenses and take advantage of him.

"By the way, this week's column is a good one. Take out the hankies," Walter said, rubbing his hands together. "My peeps will lap up this one."

The Searchlight staff in general had grown weary of Walter. From checking his mail and borrowing petty cash to pinching a sales rep's ass, Walter was an accepted part of life at the office. In the passive-aggressive spirit of the Pacific Northwest, the staff minimized contact without telling him to stop. The sales rep whose ass was pinched eventually complained to the editor after Walter had slipped her a scrap of paper on which he scribbled a phone number and "Call Daddy."

Ernest, with his inherent need to be liked, treated every-one with open arms, from the rich and trendy to the tired and poor. In that weakness, Walter mined success. Walter and the editor were more de facto friends, sharing a love for knowledge and controversy. The difference was that the editor watched from the sidelines. Walter was the cannonball who could light his own fuse.

The newspaper paid this homeless man twenty-five bucks a column. That hardly compensated for all the readers he brought to the paper, literally overnight. Ernest sometimes felt like he made a deal with the devil. The deal now included a course of action, such as calling Harold Wadsworth in case Walter died.

--

Walter strolled into the Paragon Hotel, a franchise with clean rooms and clean sheets, to meet up with Candy for a special occasion: her birthday.

All sex aside, he actually liked Candy. Since his divorce, Candy was the first woman who made Walter want to change.

"You can sign as many marriage licenses as you want," Walter once wrote. "You can go through as many wedding ceremonies as you need. You can live with as many partners as you can handle. But in the end, the best match always wins. There will always be the one we're meant to match."

At least Walter was interested in talking with Candy. A true friendship had blossomed. Walter felt more comfortable around Candy than any other woman since his divorce.

In this relationship, Walter was more open with his feel-ings and desires. Two to three nights a week, he whipped Candy as she ate from a dog dish. Among other things. He also took her to dinner at least one night a week. She liked dining at the Olive Garden. On the occasion when he paid the dinner tab, it meant he slept on the bus for an extra night or two. However, this became less of a problem as Walter got better at leveraging his columnist status to score cash from the movers and shakers and readers in Lakehaven. He still sold Oxioids on the bus or to his neighbors at the motels where he and Candy often ended up.

The last time they got together, Walter experienced a new-found jealousy over her shift at the massage parlor.

"I need to go," said Candy, nibbling on Walter's ear.

"Be good," he said. "Don't let a rich peckerwood steal you away from me."

"I'll be good, Daddy. I'll be good."

Walter knew she banged other guys, occasionally, for money. Candy knew that Walter paid other girls, often, for sex. Their conversations about staying faithful were terms of endearment.

"As a wise man once said," Walter wrote, "you can't change a tiger's stripes. You can only give him a bath."

There was one long-standing behavior, however, that threatened to send his bliss with Candy down the same destitute path as his marriage to Rose.

Walter's prescription painkiller habit stemmed from a broken foot several years earlier, but long after he kicked heroin.

As he waited for Candy, Walter ate a bowl of lukewarm oatmeal from the Paragon Hotel's continental breakfast bar. Then he gobbled three fifteen-milligram Oxioids. An hour later, his mind and body turned to jelly. A big, sloppy bowl of black jelly. The world slowed as opiates massaged his brain. He fought the urge to nod off.

Candy arrived in a tight sweater and spike heels, ready to party. Her red toenails sparkled as her stilettos click-clacked through the hotel lobby. Walter sat with his elbows on a table in the cafe, head in his hands.

"You OK, sweetie?" She tried to hug him and he half-hugged her back, a dab of drool in the corner of his mouth.

She leaned close, put a hand on his arm and whispered, "How many did you take?"

He didn't answer.

"Have you eaten? Let's go eat. Maybe you'll feel better?"

He nodded with droopy eyes. They walked out of the lobby and climbed into Candy's clean Toyota Prius. As the pale blue car left the hotel parking lot, Walter vomited out the window, leaving streaks of oats and bile down the passenger side door. He vomited on the dashboard and passed out. It was noon.

Hours later, alone in his pinstripe suit with a loosened tie and blurry vision, Walter tripped through the automatic sliding glass doors at the Paragon Hotel. He lacked a reservation, but he wanted to shower. He needed to shower. Walter swiped a phony key card and made his way to the showers at the indoor pool. He stripped naked and turned the shower dial halfway to hot.

The warm water released the tension in his head, neck, shoulders and back. He felt relaxed and dizzy, breathing through his mouth, eyes closed and head hanging low.

Walter leaned against the cold tile wall with open palms, then turned around and slid toward the waterlogged tile floor with minimal friction between his back and the wall on his way down. The warm shower sprayed his lower half. He opened and closed his knees in rhythm, the water intermittently washing his inner thighs. He gripped his erection and drowned in a dream about spanking two Asian hookers at the massage parlor.

The simultaneous gasp of horrified twin 12-year-old girls snapped Walter awake. He wiped his wet eyes and struggled to focus. The girls, who had snuck out of their hotel room for a swim, discovered a naked black man jerking off in the shower. Mired in an opiate stupor, he shielded his private parts in a quasi-standing fetal position. He pleaded for the girls to be quiet.

The girls shrieked down the hallway. Walter slipped backward on the wet tile, landing with a thud. He found his footing, grabbed his pile of clothes and scurried toward the exit. As he approached the lobby, he saw red and blue lights flickering through the prism of glass doors, casting their hues on the front desk, floor and ceiling.

--

From the jail, Walter made one phone call.

"Damn it, what did you do now?" Joe asked. "You still owe me for bailing you out the last time."

"It's a long story."

"Well here's a short story: you need to quit those goddamn pills. They turn you into a beast."

Joe drove him to The Searchlight office with a business card for a lawyer. The charges were dropped following an eyewitness account that the cop had called Walter a nigger during the arrest.

As for the shower incident, Walter concocted an official tale. In a pre-emptive move on The Searchlight before word got around, he barged into Ernest's office.

"I need five minutes," he said, closing the door. "Please."

Ernest swiveled his chair and exhaled with strained patience.

Walter sat down and leaned forward. "I had a grand mal seizure at the Paragon Hotel swimming pool."

"A seizure? Are you all right?"

"They happen from time to time, ever since I was a boy," Walter said, clasping his hands. "I'm having some legal issues with the hotel, so I've been tied up this week. I wanted you to hear it from me first. I'll be all right."

"On an unrelated topic, we keep getting random weird phone calls from women who hate your guts," Ernest said. "We got a call on Monday from some Asian woman at a massage parlor in Seattle who screamed 'He owe me money! He owe me money!' This morning, we got a call from an anonymous woman who says that we don't know the 'real Walter,' and that you're bilking people through your column."

"Damn haters," Walter said through clenched teeth. "I bet my ex-wife is one of the callers."

"I don't give a shit who it is. If the corporate brassholes hear about it, you and your column are gone, regardless of your excuse."

"Relax," Walter said. "Everything's going to be fine."

"Just stay out of trouble, damn it. I can't go to bat for you anymore," Ernest said. "I've used all my cards."

Their friendship was an arranged marriage, equipped with a self-destruct button. Walter had long ago phased himself into Ernest's routine. He grabbed the satchel and headed for the door. "See you in the morning."

--

Joe called Ernest for a meeting and drove to the newspaper office in his smoke-filled pea green Cadillac.

Joe initially put out feelers for editorial sympathy as he mulled over a school board campaign, but the subject soon turned to Walter. They were both infected with Walter, a parasite who knew when to go dormant and when to drain the host. Joe even told Ernest about the crushed Volkswagen Rabbit.

"You knew he was homeless, right?" Joe asked, sipping coffee from a stainless steel tumbler.

"I figured he was a couch surfer, something like that,"

Ernest said. "How long has he been homeless?"

"Lord, I don't know. Six years? Ever since his divorce, I know that much," Joe said. "That's the last permanent residence he had, you see. He's been using my address."

"We get all kinds of calls from women who hate him," Ernest said. "All I know is that he milks me and the newspaper for all we're worth."

"He uses The Searchlight's address as his work address when filling out paperwork," Joe said, leaning back in the chair. "You knew that, right?"

"Doesn't surprise me. We get his junk mail," Ernest said. "I created a monster with this column. The harder I push him away, the harder he pushes back."

"There's no such thing as a little bit of Walter," Joe said. "I try to keep him at arm's length, but if you crack the door just a hair, he comes flooding in like a goddamn tsunami."

"I can only take him in small doses," Ernest said. "It's like I have no choice. He's a part of my work routine whether I like it or not."

"I know one thing," Joe said. "He loves writing that column. It's all he talks about. That and his daughter."

"He takes up more of my time than my staff. The sports editor told me, when I first started this job, to watch out for Walter: 'He'll sink his talons into you and won't let go.' Why didn't I listen?"

"Readers love him," Joe said. "Everyone else knows he's full of shit."

"And those people," Ernest said, "still read every word."

Spokane, WA

In the comfort of her family room with a crackling fireplace, Rose thumbed through The Searchlight, her petite bare feet propped on a brown leather ottoman.

"Mom," she said to Grandma, who sat in the adjacent recliner, knitting a powder blue sweater. "Did you read about naked man at the Paragon Hotel?"

Rose recited the lead item in the police blotter:

> At approximately 10:21 p.m. Saturday in the 34000 block of Foster Street, police responded to a call about a naked man in the Paragon Hotel's pool area. According to the police, two juveniles found the man sleeping naked in the shower. Multiple units were called to the scene to arrest the suspect, who appeared intoxicated and was knocking on the doors of hotel guests. Police took the man into custody without incident.

"That happened at the Paragon? Good grief," Grandma said, tilting her head back and smiling. "Your father and I would stay at the Paragon for weekend getaways. Do they still have hot tubs in the rooms? We liked to cuddle in the hot tub. Oooh, that was so much fun."

"I don't need that mental image of you and dad," Rose said. "That's super gross."

"It's better than picturing a naked loon in the shower," Grandma said. "You know, all I ever read about in the newspaper is all these loonies in Lakehaven. This city has gone downhill. It makes Detroit look like Disneyland."

"I worry about raising Lilly here. Plus I need to get the hell away from Walter."

"Can't blame you, sweetheart," Grandma said. "Are you still hunting for jobs?"

"Yes, but no luck," Rose said, folding the newspaper in her lap. "I need to get the hell out of Lakehaven and the Seattle area in general. I can't go anywhere without being reminded of Walter. It's like I've been branded with a big red W in the middle of my forehead."

"Dear, it can't be that bad."

"Did I tell you about the teachers at school who think Walter's column is some kind of godsend for education?"

"You've got be kidding me. That drivel?"

"I'm dead serious, mom. They have no clue what he's really like. Not one damn clue."

"Have you told them?"

"What's the use? I've seen the letters in the paper, saying how he 'tells it like it is' and how he's a 'breath of fresh air for Lakehaven schools.' It makes me sick. Just plain sick."

"You still have to deal with him because of Lilly."

"He sets a bad example for my daughter."

"That's true," Grandma said. "But she does love her father, whether you like it or not."

"Mom, don't do this to me," Rose said. "It irritates me when you defend Walter."

"Honey, he will always be Lilly's father, no matter how much you hate him. You can't take that away from Lilly," Grandma said. "Besides, why waste your energy on him?"

"The courts require us to live in the state," said Rose, glancing out the window. "My friend in Spokane said the schools are hiring."

"Why don't you give it a try? At the very least, you won't be force-fed that daily dose of Walter."

To Rose's delight, the courts eventually suspended Walter's right to visit with his daughter until he completed a mental evaluation and a state-sponsored program on alcohol abuse.

Walter soon learned that Lilly was moving to Spokane because Rose had accepted a teaching job. Rose's attorney mailed this information to Walter, who picked up his mail at Joe's house. Walter wadded up the letter after reading it twice. He thought of the snow-caked Cascade mountain passes in the wintertime.

"Spokane," he said, shaking his head, a copy of The Searchlight under his arm. "Of all places, Spokane."

Five minutes

Walter showed up at the editor's office, unannounced as usual. The receptionist was on her coffee break, hence the absence of a buffer.

"I've got a hot one here," said Walter, dropping a spiral-bound notebook on the desk.

"We already typed your column for this week," Ernest said. "I don't have time this morning."

"Are you busy now?"

"I need to get this shit done before a meeting in twenty minutes," Ernest said, shuffling papers at his desk.

"Give me just five minutes," he said, louder.

"Walter, I'd - "

"Five minutes," he said, louder.

"Fine." Ernest rolled his eyes and swiveled toward the monitor.

Walter rubbed his hands like an excited kid at Christmas about to unwrap a gift. His public speaking voice, already smooth and commanding, was temporarily free from the pill-induced slur.

"This one's called 'The Poison Apple of Education.' You like the title?"

"I think you're a poison apple," Ernest said.

Walter grinned with intent to disarm. His teeth twinkled. The editor pursed his lips and typed.

"I am a parent who cares about the future of our children's education," Walter said, pacing with the notebook. "I am a simple person, with chores and bills. I contribute to society. I love my family. But when my child's basic education needs aren't being met, I have a problem."

The editor typed with blurry fingers.

"When the state fails to provide adequate funding for my child's school, she suffers. When my child suffers, the rest of her family suffers. There are thousands of families affected by Lakehaven schools, which means there are thousands of families with children who suffer."

Walter repeated that last line as Ernest caught up.

"The legislative bureaucrats have hogtied and gagged Lakehaven schools. That's right. They tied our wrists behind our backs, linked them to our ankles, then stuffed sweaty gym socks in our mouths."

Ernest paused, shook his head and resumed pecking at the keyboard.

"Thank God for leaders like Lakehaven School District Superintendent Harvey Oakes, who lobbies on behalf of our children and our city. Bless the teachers who enrich our children through creativity and tough love. Remember, it's OK for a child to finish last in a race, and it's OK if only the first-place winners receive a trophy.

"I fantasize about what our education system could be. I dream of a school system where all means all. I long to see every parent involved in Lakehaven schools. I hope for one-hundred percent graduation rates, and I pray that each and every one of our children becomes a lifelong learner.

"You might say my dream is naive. But I refuse to let today's education system feed poison apples to our children. I will find a solution. I will pursue that dream and find the lighthouse at the edge of darkness. I will follow the light, step by step, closer and closer, mile by mile. I will reach the lighthouse, even if I reach it alone."

There was silence until Ernest caught up.

"This is where I get stuck," Walter said, slapping his lap with the notebook. "I can't think of an ending."

"Wrap it up like one of your school board speeches," Ernest said.

Walter cleared his throat and resumed his smooth baritone.

"If we don't stand up for the children, who will? My fellow parents, we have a job to do. Let's do it right."

He waited for Ernest to finish.

"Well?"

"Good stuff," said Ernest, who glanced at his watch. The session lasted a hair longer than five minutes.

"Thank you," Walter said, grabbing his satchel and tipping his white cap. "You have a good day."

--

Walter's columns continued to work miracles.

"When I hit rock bottom, I told God, if you don't save me, you're going to lose me," Walter said while riding in Ernest's Jeep. "Three days later, I was in your office."

They drove to the Christian television station WJCC on Lakehaven's southern end. The station manager had booked Walter as a guest on "Town Talk," which aired every Sunday.

"They want me to talk about education," Walter said, gazing out the filmy window at the sunrise that backlighted the Cascade mountains coated in wispy fingers of fog. Warm air gushed full throttle from a vent at Walter's feet.

"Is this a TV show for holy rollers?" Ernest asked.

"Now, now - don't be hating."

"At least I keep my superstitions private."

"Listen, I'd rather believe and find out I was wrong than not believe and find out they were right."

The Lakehaven station was an affiliate of a national network. The host, Guy Petty, invited Walter after reading his columns about education.

They waited in the lobby. Walter adjusted his tie and collar on his pinstripe suit. Ernest clutched a coffee cup.

"Hello, gentlemen," said Guy Petty, shaking hands with Walter and Ernest. He led them to the green room behind the stage. On the formica table was a stack of Walter's articles clipped from The Searchlight.

"First of all, I want you to know that Ernest Handsy is the one who breathes life into my prose," Walter said. "Without him, I am nothing."

"Aw, come on," said Ernest, who heard a hint of slur in Walter's voice. "I just dot the i's and cross the t's."

"You write with such gravity," Guy Petty said, turning to Walter. The host was a rebel among the network's station managers because he discussed secular topics and spared the prayers. His jaw moved like a ventriloquist doll's mouth when he laughed.

They entered a gymnasium-like room with a high ceiling and a slate floor. On the stage were two leather sofas surrounded on all sides by microphones, cameras, hot lights, plastic flowers, a fireplace and all the fixings of the average senior's living room.

Petty gave Walter a few pointers as a makeup artist powdered their faces.

"Stand up and hold the back of your coat as you sit down," Petty demonstrated. "There, it feels uncomfortable, but your collar hangs better that way."

With the cameras rolling, Walter defended his positions on education in Lakehaven.

"At the root of the problem," he said, "is the lack of parental participation."

"You are known for making that point in your columns," Guy Petty said. "For the viewers at home, please expand on that point."

"As a father, I have a moral duty to raise a confident and well adjusted child," Walter said. "I must set an example."

"Amen," said the host, rocking back and forth in his seat.

"I have seen the graduation rates and dropout rates of Lakehaven students. Any investment a parent makes toward the education of their child is a wise investment."

Walter sat sharp in his suit and tie, conversing like a gentleman for the viewers at home. The viewers at home approved. The TV camera showed Walter as a respectable, morally responsible citizen who contributed to society.

--

A week later, Walter invited Guy Petty to coffee at the Village Diner on a drizzly morning.

"Thanks again for having me on your show," Walter said.

"We enjoyed having you," Guy said. "Any discussion about education is a discussion worth having."

The waitress topped off their coffee mugs.

"How's your daughter?" asked Guy, warming his hands on the ceramic mug.

"Lilly is doing well. Got straight A's on her last report card."

"You must be a proud papa," Guy said, stirring his coffee with a fork. "I'll bet she's smart like her Daddy."

"I do my best as a single father to give her what she needs."

"Do you have custody?"

"She lives with her mother. I see her as much as I can."

"I'll bet that's tough," Guy said. "My kids are like a drug. Even though they're all grown up, I can't get enough of them. And my grandkids? Whew! They're something else, all four of them. I am truly blessed."

"I work hard," Walter said, "but you know how it is, trying to make ends meet, struggling just to pay the rent."

"I sure do," Guy said, adjusting the strap of the sandal on his white-socked foot. "I was homeless for almost three years."

Walter was stunned into stillness.

"It's true. In my thirties, I was a meth addict," Guy said. "I lost my wife, my job, even my teeth." He grinned and tapped his index finger on his false front incisors. "Thank God for the TV station. I sobered up and the station hired me as a janitor. That was almost three decades ago."

"I have a whole new sense of respect for you," Walter said. "I'll bet that's why there's no nonsense about your show."

"Between you and I, this station gets away with a lot. Much more than the satellite channels in the Midwest and South."

"You mean flyover country?"

"Indeed. The West Coast is more relaxed. Everyone has more freedom. Or at least it feels that way."

"It's more live and let live," Walter said. "I just focus on providing for my daughter. It's tough to get her everything she needs."

"Is she OK?"

"She's not starving," Walter said. "But there is a struggle to get her the basics. Like shoes. She's worn the same pair of sneakers for a year. The soles are taped together. That kind of thing."

"I know how fast kids go through shoes," Guy said. "Raised three daughters myself."

"If I save through the end of winter, I should be able to - ."

"Walter," said Guy, putting a hand on his shoulder. "I

want to help you."

Guy pulled a Benjamin Franklin out of his wallet.

"Are you sure?" Walter said, taking the money. "Please, you don't have to do this."

"Walter," Guy said. "I'll always help an honest man."

--

That afternoon, in the courtyard at Mount Rainier Elementary School, Walter spotted a stocky man in a red running suit with white stripes lining the length of his arms and legs. A silver coach's whistle gleamed in the sun as it dangled from a shoelace looped around the man's hairy neck.

The man in the red and white striped running suit kept his scalp shaved clean and wore a white terry cloth headband. He consoled a crying boy as they walked toward the office. The man ran his clawed fingers up and down the boy's back in a nurturing manner. He glanced up and caught Walter's stare. He nodded a stranger's greeting and entered the building.

Walter saw Lilly trotting through the saturated moss-coated grass toward him. She wrapped her arms around Daddy.

"Who's that guy in the red running suit who just walked in that door?" asked Walter, pointing.

"That's Mr. Hudson. He's the gym teacher."

"Is he a good guy?"

"Sort of," Lilly said. "His thumb looks like a toe. Plus he makes me run the whole mile. He won't let me skip any laps."

"You need to run all your laps. Exercise is good for you, baby girl."

"But I hate running!" she said, cheeks flushed red from running to her father. "I always get really out of breath and then I always finish last. I hate it."

"Listen, you need to follow instructions from Mr. Hudson and run your laps," Walter said, holding her arm tight. "But don't ever be alone with him. You got that?"

She nodded.

"Ever. I mean it."

"OK. Why?"

"There's something about him I don't trust. Sometimes fathers just have a feeling about these things. And while we're on the topic of safety," he said as they turned toward the sandwich joint, "stay away from drugs. They'll ruin your life."

She nodded.

"Got that? Drugs will ruin your life. Look me in the eyes and tell me you'll stay away from drugs."

"OK, Daddy, I'll stay away from drugs. Drugs are stupid."

"I'm just looking out for my baby girl," Walter said, putting an arm around Lilly. "It's a nasty, violent and unforgiving world out there."

He's My Dad

The all-night bus crawled from Lakehaven through every city in the county, turned around in downtown Seattle and returned to Lakehaven, seven days a week.

In all, the trip lasted six hours. About forty people booked their motel on wheels. With a few pills to hustle, Walter arrived early to guarantee a seat for the night. His wet sneakers squeaked on the steps as he boarded. He greeted the pot-bellied factory foreman who moonlighted as the bus driver, several nights a week, to help feed a family of nine.

Most passengers stared straight ahead as he shuffled down the aisle, stepping on flattened segments of straw wrappers. On this night, he snagged an unoccupied seat in the back row. He brushed away a wadded tissue and tucked his leather satchel and garment bag in the corner. He sipped a margarita-in-a-can, still cold from the convenience store cooler.

The driver dimmed the lights and cranked up the heat as the crowded rig chugged out of Lakehaven toward the mighty ports of Seattle. Rain pounded the roof and windows.

Walter jumped awake every few minutes in fight-or-flight mode before dozing back to a mixed-dream state. The longest stretch of sleep was an intense twenty minutes. The padded seats reeked of dirty bodies, but provided more cushion than the floor mats at any homeless shelter. Everyone kept to themselves, and the price of the ticket was a bargain. The homeless population packed every mission in the county, especially in winter, when the overnight weather flirted with freezing temperatures.

This bus was a shiver-free bus, all year long.

When the doors squeaked open at the end of the line, Walter was already dressed for the day, satchel and garment bag over his shoulder. He stepped off the bus and into the pre-dawn fog, filling his lungs with moist air. He straightened his white baseball hat and sought refuge in the nearest coffee shop. The roasted coffee aroma pried open his bloodshot eyes, and the smiling blonde barista sweetened the morning by batting her long eyelashes. He scooted a metal chair up to the corner table and unfolded a white sheet of notebook paper with ragged edges. It was a poem Lilly had written.

He's My Dad
By Lilly Wadsworth, fifth grade

He taught me to read, he taught me to write
He made sure I knew what was wrong and right
He lives somewhere else, and it makes me sad
Because I'm his daughter, and he's my dad

He's smart and funny and listens so well
I can share a secret, and he won't tell
I miss him so much, and it makes me sad
Because I'm his daughter, and he's my dad

He walks on water, he walks on air
He's with me every night in prayer
He's not there, and it makes me sad
Because I'm his daughter, and he's my dad

Our time together means the world to me
He always takes me seriously
I still get to see him, and that's not so bad
Because I'm his daughter, and he's my dad

I look like my dad, we have the same eyes
We have the same laugh, the same look of surprise
I'll make him proud of the child he had
Because I'm his daughter, and he's my dad

--

Walter liked Ernest's idea of compiling his columns into a book.

"I've never produced a book before," Ernest said. "Might be a good way to boost both of our credentials."

"You have my permission to start right away," Walter said. "How much do you think it could sell?"

"A few hundred or a few thousand copies, who knows?" Ernest said. "The latter would get a publishing house's attention."

"We should self-publish the book. Skip the middle man."

"That's what I was thinking," Ernest said. "I found a small print shop in Olympia. The owner said he could print the books at four dollars each. That's a lot cheaper than The Searchlight's presses."

"How much would it sell for?"

"I was thinking fifteen bucks a copy," Ernest said. "If we sell a thousand copies, that's ten-grand in profit. I bet we could do it."

The possibility of striking gold made Walter lightheaded as his eyes glowed with green dollar symbols.

"Never in my career have I seen a column get the kind

of feedback that you get, week after week," Ernest said. "We would be crazy not to try. Let's see what happens. At the very least, you'll have a book to shop around."

Walter exhaled and rubbed his hands together. "A book," he said, shaking his head. "I never thought in a million years that I would write a book, or that I was already writing one."

Walter's weekly rock star role at The Searchlight felt like a divine calling. The book was a natural next step.

"I couldn't have done it without you," he told Ernest in a compliment as sincere as a child's smile.

Walter fantasized about propping his slippered feet up on a desk, wearing a charcoal Armani suit and a Rolex, smoking a Cuban cigar, with a brunette on each side, driving a Bentley with tinted windows and shiny rims, parking at a waterfront mansion with a warm bed and a harem of women waiting for him to come home.

He also dreamed about funding Lilly's tuition at an Ivy League university. This dream ignited his fatherly instincts to provide and protect.

--

The next morning at eight o'clock sharp, with his fatherly instincts on fire, Walter barged into Ernest's office.

"Let's get coffee. My treat."

They climbed into Ernest's green Jeep, and upon leaving Sassy Espresso, Walter said they needed to pick up Lilly.

Ernest rolled his eyes as Walter milked another favor. He should have known better because there's no such thing as a little bit of Walter, and with every favor, there's a catch.

"Park here," Walter said, motioning to the curb near the back corner of the house, out of view from the front porch.

Walter knocked on the oak door and waited for Lilly to come out. Rose did not allow him in the house. This was the same ex-wife who called The Searchlight, begging the paper to quit running Walter's column, insisting that "the columns are complete bullshit" and that Walter "is a waste of a man."

Ernest thought of that phone call as he sat in the idling Jeep. Walter and Lilly appeared from around a bush.

"Where did you get your new shoes?" Walter asked as he eyeballed Lilly's spotless basketball sneakers.

"I got them at the mall," she said. "Do you like them?"

"They look expensive. Did your mother buy them?"

"Yeah. They were on sale. What do you think?"

"They're nice, baby girl." Walter wished he would have bought those sneakers.

He pulled the passenger seat forward and Lilly climbed into the back seat. He directed his chauffeur/editor to a nearby park. Ernest brought a camera, as requested. This was the first time Ernest had heard of Lilly's poetry book or a plan to produce her poetry book.

"Make her look like a distinguished author," Walter said. Lilly's book was a compilation of her poems including "A Nose For Friends" and "He's My Dad." It was her proud father's idea. All the poems were stapled together and printed in pencil on ragged-edged notebook paper.

Silly season

Every autumn, the Lakehaven gossip mill referred to elections as the Silly Season. Tensions ripened over the summer until humans and politicians howled at the moon. The political quicksand sucked up thousands of dollars in donations and ads. Candidates bombarded every mailbox and kissed every Searchlight reporter's ass.

The legend in Lakehaven was that Silly Season began with the first full moon in September. The moon triggered the tides of Puget Sound and awakened the beasts. Violence spiked in the days when the moon was at its peak in the autumn months, or so the headlines suggested. One story reported that assaults and rapes increased dramatically between Labor Day and Election Day.

The transition from summer to fall heightened the impulses, especially in people who had difficulty reigning them in. Of the creatures in this story, Walter was the most impulsive. The pills illustrated this well enough. His cravings and tolerance intensified bit by bit, accumulated over several years. The buzz was less enjoyable and more functional.

The habit got expensive when he was undercut by a new dealer in the market, and the bus passengers were scoring pills at the homeless shelter in Seattle.

Through his column in The Searchlight over the past year, Walter had farmed a fertile field of readers willing to loan a few dollars here and there. As the addiction deepened daily, he strategized his sources of income and status. Joe and Ernest supplied some life support, but Walter needed bigger fish, or at least any fish who were willing to bite. Walter's survival strategy in the suburban jungle underwent a metamorphosis at the start of this particular Silly Season, much in the same way the nights grew longer, the birds flew south, and the breeze transitioned from a brush to a nip.

Walter sat on the concrete bench at the bus shelter with a copy of The Searchlight. The outstretched newspaper fluttered in the breeze.

After reading his latest column, Walter flipped back to the front page. In the lower righthand corner was a story about a Lakehaven-born scientist who had programmed NASA's most recent robotic rover on Mars. The reporter noted the scientist was an Eagle Scout, a master outdoorsman and a devout Mormon. On page two was a group photo of ten teenagers who earned Eagle Scout status. The caption noted that all ten boys were honor students and members of the Church of Jesus Christ of Latter-day Saints. Walter scribbled a point about Mormons in his spiral notebook and resumed reading the newspaper.

On page three was a short item about candidates in the fall election. So far, Christian Castle Pastor Levi Cooke was running unopposed for state representative, while Joe Lippy had filed to run for the school board against incumbent Ted Farley. Walter shook his head and turned the page.

On page four was a photo of a poker-faced Lakehaven man being led from the courtroom in shackles after a judge sentenced him to five years in prison for molesting a prepubescent niece. Walter clenched his teeth in silent rage.

--

The next morning, Walter crossed the street to The Searchlight office, exhausted from the night's sins. His head throbbed, his mouth was dry, and he had no money.

The employee lounge had turbo-strength coffee on tap. The first sip kicked his body into gear, and the second sip helped wash down a pill.

With coffee cup in hand, he strolled through the news-room's chorus of typing reporters. He sniffed the air's linger-ing ink chemicals on his way to the editor's office, only to find the lights out.

"When does Ernest get back?" Walter asked the reception-ist. "This is important."

"He's out for the day," she replied, engrossed in a game of solitaire.

"May I please leave a message?"

The receptionist futzed around the desk for a pen and paper. "I'll tell him you stopped by."

What he really needed was ten dollars and a ride to the pharmacy. He chugged the coffee and set the mug on the receptionist's desk. Walter embarked for the library, trotting at a steady gait as the wind and rain pounded him all over. A strong gust nearly blew the white cap off his head. Endless traffic streamed by on Foster Street with every vehicle's wind-shield wipers going full speed.

Tuesdays were always busy at the library, and this day was no different. Every computer station was booked, with the last two spots swiped by a pair of Mormon males in white short sleeves, ties and name tags.

Soaked from the rain, Walter sat down at a table. He pulled out a spiral notebook and black pen from his satchel. The notebook was open to a blank page with the title printed in black.

Let's send the Mormons to Mars
By Walter Wadsworth, Searchlight columnist

Ask yourself the following:
Why do hotel maids speak Spanish?
Have you ever met a poor Jew?
Why do Asians run the nail salons?
When will white guys learn to dance?
Where are all the black hockey players?
Stereotypes tell the truth. Indeed, my Jewish friends are well connected, my Latino friends are great gardeners, my white friends have no rhythm, and my black friends have no money.

Which brings us to Mormonism, the most stereotyped and misunderstood religion in the country. Mormons live in their own world and march to the beat of their own drum. The Book of Mormon even describes a Mormon planet called Kolob. With a dark past of polygamy that thrives in a few fringe sects, the Latter-day Saints (LDS) are scorned by Christians and secular folks alike.

I am not a Mormon. Never have been, never will be. No magic underwear for this black man. And contrary to those LDS-sponsored billboards along the freeway, I have never met a black Mormon.

That said, I want to set the record straight: one day, the Mormons may come to our rescue.

Love them or hate them, Mormons offer hope for the human race. I ask the enemies of Mormons to please lend me your ears, for I know a way to rid the planet of these people. To the Mormons themselves, please pay attention, for you will one day save us all. The solution is a win-win for everybody.

Let's send the Mormons to Mars.

The mainstream media buzzes with the possibility of sending a man to Mars.

Make no mistake, society has benefited from space endeavors. In the 1960s, the Space Race bent and stretched humanity's boundaries. Innovations ranging from dried food to telecommunications all owed their impetus to the Space Race, which stemmed from the Cold War nuclear arms buildup between the U.S. and the Soviets.

Today, the war is between the people and the planet. While we're busy destroying the Earth, we must find a new planet to pollute.

I don't mean to sound like a namby-pamby tree-hugger, but I want my daughter - and future grandchildren - to inherit a healthy planet from their forefathers.

If we want a healthier human race, and we plan to colonize Mars, then let's send the Mormons. To explain this theory, let's consider all the stereotypes.

First of all, the family unit is the focus. Mormons live clean and clear-headed. They avoid coffee, booze and tobacco.

Mormons are self-sufficient and work hard. Church leader Brigham Young, along with his wives and followers, created Salt Lake City. Through ingenuity and irrigation, these pioneers turned the arid Utah wasteland into a thriving settlement. They built a community from scratch.

Educators know that Mormons take academics seriously. Mormons believe in hard work, and as the stereotype goes, they don't do anything halfway. In other words, they do things right.

There are 14 million Mormons worldwide. That's more than the population of New York City, Los Angeles and Seattle combined.

As a group, the stereotype says they behave in lock-step. Get one on board, and the rest will follow.

Honorable mention for the first humans to colonize Mars would go to the Amish. I suppose the Mormons get the nod, however, because of their ability to adapt to the times. One can follow the Mormon virtues of honest work and healthy families without resorting to magic underwear. But if magic underwear is what it takes to reach humanity's potential beyond this planet, then so be it.

My reason for writing this column has nothing to do with space or religion. It has everything to do with my primary muse - education. The Mormons know that education is a cornerstone of healthy families and a higher quality of life. That should be their stereotype. The Mormons follow that ideal as part of their faith, even if they clash with your overall worldview. The virtues of education are intertwined with their worldview. How about yours?

Send the Mormons to Mars. Let them build another Salt Lake City on the Red Planet. Let them turn another desert into their dreams. Let the Mormons lead the way beyond Earth, when the time comes. The rest of us just might follow.

--

That afternoon, upon typing the last word of Walter's ode to Mormon stereotypes, Ernest took off his glasses and rubbed his eyes.

"We can't print this," Ernest said.

"Why not?"

"Readers will find it offensive."

"Not if they read the whole thing," Walter said, knowing that readers would read up to the last word. "Everything I write is true."

"How the hell does this even relate to Lakehaven?" Ernest said. "This doesn't relate to current education issues, either."

"This has everything to do with Lakehaven and education," Walter said. "Don't you agree that everyone could learn from the Mormons? They could educate the rest of us."

"I guess."

"Right!" Walter said. "Just like my peeps."

"Just like your peeps."

"So you'll print it?"

"I'm going to catch a lot of shit over this," Ernest said, sighing. "One of my bosses is a Mormon. I once saw his magic underwear. Don't ask me how."

"Last time I checked, The Searchlight was the gold standard for freedom of speech in Lakehaven," Walter said. "Your boss will get over it."

--

Over the summer, and to Walter's surprise, Joe Lippy had entered the race for Lakehaven School Board at the last minute. As the biggest thorn in the school board's ass, Joe sparked a storm of chatter over what he would do, if elected. Parents and administrators immediately endorsed the incumbent, Ted Farley, to keep Joe from stealing the seat.

Joe placed campaign signs around town. The signs were neon yellow with "Education first: Vote for Joe Lippy" written in English and Korean.

On his rusty pea green Cadillac's passenger door was a placemat-sized magnet version of the campaign sign.

"We couldn't ask for better fall weather," Joe said as Walter strolled into the open garage. Their eyes were bloodshot from pills and booze. "Now let's go shoot some guns."

The Cadillac scooted along Marine View Drive, hugging the shoulder, windows open, Walter's open palm outside the window, pushing the air. The old Lakehaven lighthouse was visible in the distance, overlooking the Sound and standing tall in direct sunlight.

"I brought my new .44-Magnum," Joe said, shifting gears with his right hand, left hand on the wheel, pipe in his mouth. The tobacco smoke streamed out the window.

"I didn't grow up around guns," Walter said as the pills started to slow his head.

"Well then," Joe said, laughing and coughing. "Looks like we're going to man you up."

"Look, there's a Ted Farley campaign sign," Walter said, pointing at a placard on a stake in a pocket of grass.

"The difference between his signs and my signs," Joe said, "is that my signs have a strategy behind them."

He referred to the message in English and Korean.

"Do the Koreans actually vote in elections?" Walter asked.

"People will do anything a sign tells them to do."

"Not necessarily," Walter said. "Besides, Ted Farley has a lock on the old voters, and old people vote."

It was true. Farley owned a successful auto parts store and had a history of service in Lakehaven. Farley was an elder at the Lakehaven Church of Jesus Christ of Latter-Day Saints. There weren't a lot of Mormons in Lakehaven, but there were enough, and they voted.

"Ted Farley is going to need all the magic underwear he can get because I'm going to whip the pants off him," said Joe, driving through a stop sign near his house. "I'll recruit enough Koreans in Lakehaven to make this a competitive race."

"The Koreans don't give a shit about local government or the schools," Walter said. "You're wasting your time."

"Bullshit! Koreans make up a decent chunk of Lakehaven. About twelve percent. They're an untapped resource," Joe said. "Now if only I could speak Korean."

Joe fumbled through the glove box in the Cadillac. "Take a look at this ad I'm putting in The Searchlight," he said, yanking out a sheet of paper that looked identical to the campaign signs and the magnet on his car door.

They parked in a handicapped spot at the Lakehaven Shooting Range. The two o's in the word "shooting" on the outdoor sign were shaped like targets.

A row of ten numbered booths lined the garage-like shooting room, steeped in the perfume of fresh gunpowder. At the last booth, with bullets spread out on a carpeted ledge, Joe adjusted his safety glasses and ear protection. He inserted the phallic bullets, aimed the .44 Magnum at the paper bull's eye, and pulled the trigger until it clicked.

Boom! His arm bucked with each shot, orange fireworks flashing off the barrel, filling the booth with metallic smoke.

"That, my friend, is a fucking gun," said Joe, grabbing a handful of bullets. He gestured to Walter. "Let's man you up."

Walter adjusted the noise-muffling headphones and his safety glasses. He gripped the gun with both hands. The adrenaline surged in his veins, gushing from every gland, heightened awareness to the max.

Boom! The thunderous shot blasted the human silhouette on the paper target in the distance. Walter's hands vibrated as if he had struck a steel pole with a baseball bat. He finally lost his firearms virginity, deflowered by Joe's gunpowder.

"Curiously satisfying," Walter said, grinning as they left.

Joe smiled, pulled the pipe from his mouth and exhaled.

"You see, man was meant to be armed. A wolverine can slash with its claws, right? A skunk can spray its musk, right?" said Joe, his hair blowing from the open car window. "A man should be able to arm himself. It's in the Constitution!"

Joe shifted gears as they cruised the highway along Puget Sound. The evergreen carpeted islands and the Olympic Mountains hypnotized all drivers on the highway into driving at the same speed. That's how tranquil and clear the view was on this cruise in Joe's Cadillac.

Joe puffed the vanilla tobacco in his pipe while shifting into fourth gear and launching a discussion on persuasive writing.

"Now the reader can smell bullshit a mile away, you see. Emotions are the one thing all humans share," Joe said. "We express them to different degrees, but each emotion affects the body's stress signals in the same way, thus creating a familiar response."

Joe puffed some more. Walter said "Hmm" and "I see" intermittently.

"All you need is the guts to say what needs to be said, you see," Joe said. "The right answer always wins."

"Joe," Walter said, "can you drive me to the motel?"

--

The next afternoon, Walter walked up to the window at Joe's house and said hello.

Joe shrieked and clutched his chest. "Damn it, knock at the front door!"

Walter squeezed through the bookshelves and piles to reach Joe's corner by the window. Paperwork from a children's foundation covered the desk. Those orphans from the TV commercials poked at Joe's soft spots. Joe agreed to sponsor a child for twenty dollars a month. The child lived in Costa Rica, according to the foundation - a brown shaggy-haired 10-year-old boy with a dirty face.

"I have Lilly for the weekend. Can I borrow ten dollars?"

Without saying a word, Joe held his smoldering pipe in one hand and got out his wallet.

"Thank you. I appreciate it," Walter said, folding the bills and stuffing them into his front pocket. "By the way, I heard a rumor that The Searchlight is going to endorse Ted Farley for school board."

"I'm not surprised," Joe said. He shrugged, wiped his nose and puffed his pipe. "They always go with the status quo. The problem, you see, is that they don't have the balls to advocate for real change."

"You definitely have an uphill battle," Walter said.

"The voters want a safe choice, you see. The status quo feels threatened by someone who tells it like it is."

That night, tucked inside his cave, Joe positioned a book-sized mirror on the desk and rehearsed his stump speech.

"Remember the time when Ted Farley cared about quality education?" he said, pausing for drama. "Neither do I."

Joe laughed as he looked in the mirror and said to himself, "I'm starting to sound like Walter." Joe's eyes shifted in the reflection to a photo pinned on a bulletin board behind him. His grin faded. Joe and the boy in the photo had the same grin. That boy in the photo was his son, Robert, pictured at age twelve.

Joe put down the speech and uncorked a bottle of wine as he pictured his son as a grown man. Robert lived in West Palm Beach, Florida, about the farthest from Lakehaven as one could get in the continental U.S. They hadn't spoken since Robert was eighteen, when he shipped off to San Antonio for boot camp. Joe assumed his son didn't want him in his life after such a turbulent upbringing.

Joe was right.

There was a brief spell, about ten years ago, where they corresponded. Robert reached out to Joe, having found his phone number. They swapped stories about the barracks and army hijinks. They talked about the weather. The connection was a lamp in the darkest corners of their lives until Robert went cold after becoming a father himself.

Their last phone call ended with Robert berating Joe for neglecting the family all those years ago and choosing the bars over his own son.

In the last handwritten letter Joe ever wrote, he reached out to his son, who never wrote back:

Dear Robert,

I hope you are well. We've had one hell of a summer, nothing like I've seen since moving to the Northwest. You've probably seen on the news that we were socked with record rain over the past few weeks. Last week, the sewers flooded and turned my street into a lake.

So, how have you all been? I haven't heard from you in a while. Just hope things are OK. Besides the weather, nothing much has changed with me.

My health has improved. I'm on a vitamin plan now, and it seems to be working. My knees are still killing me, however, especially in the winter.

Lately, I've been attending Lakehaven School Board meetings. This school district is a joke. Nothing is going to change as long as all these bureaucrats are in charge. I enjoy being the fly in the status quo's ointment.

I'm sure you have more pictures of little Cory now, how about sending me a couple? I'm sure he has grown quite a bit by now. Drop me a line and let me know that you are healthy and well. I know there is some tension between us and I just hope we can work through it. We can't turn back the clock and start over, but we can move forward and get to know each other again.

I love and miss you.

Love,

Dad

Sassy Espresso

With his office door closed, Ernest typed like a madman. The editorial's title was "Vote yes for Lakehaven schools." It was an endorsement for a construction bond that sought ninety million dollars from taxpayers. Ernest swizzled coffee, adjusted his glasses, and reviewed the editorial's conclusion.

> Quality schools do more than educate our children and prepare them for tomorrow. Quality schools attract families and companies that create living-wage jobs. The Searchlight urges voters to approve the Lakehaven school bond and invest in the community's quality of life.

A knock at the door stopped Ernest's typing cold. He clenched his teeth and fists, expecting to see Walter's wide eyes and white hat in the office door.

Ernest swiveled in his chair to find the receptionist at the door.

"Walter's here to see you," she said, wrinkling her nose.

"Boy oh boy," Ernest said. He thumped his fist on the desk and rattled the clutter. "I'm surprised Walter doesn't sleep here."

"Want me to tell him you're on a conference call?"

Ernest looked behind the receptionist and saw Walter, wearing his pinstripe suit and white cap, in the distance. They made eye contact.

Ernest sighed.

"Goddamn it, send him back," he said. "But next time, please tell him I'm busy. I don't know how much longer I can tolerate him."

"Glad to play interference. That's my job," the receptionist said. No sooner had she walked away that Walter and his musk filled the room.

"I know you're busy, but this will only take a minute."

"That's what you always say," Ernest said, tossing up his hands. "Seriously, Walter. You don't need to come in here every day. You take more of my time than my employees, for crying out loud."

"Calm down, my friend. I'll be quick," said Walter, his hands in prayer position. "I'm not sure why you're treating me this way, but from now on, I will only come by to work on the column. You have my word."

Ernest nodded.

"I finally found a challenger for Levi Cooke in the Legislature race."

Ernest raised his eyebrows. "Who?"

"Geoffrey Parker."

"Who the hell is Geoffrey Parker?"

"The next state rep from Lakehaven, that's who."

"Never heard of him."

"He owns Sassy Espresso."

"You mean the coffee shop with the bikini baristas?"

Walter nodded. "I suggested he run for the position. He's got the cash."

"Let me guess," Ernest said, leaning back, folding his hands behind his head. "You're a customer at Sassy Espresso."

"As a matter of fact, those beautiful women make a fine

latte, oh yeah," Walter said, sucking air between his front teeth. "Come on. I know you've checked it out."

"Perhaps I've researched it once or twice," Ernest said. "The last time I was there, I ended up tipping the barista three bucks for a three-dollar coffee."

"Geoffrey Parker and I shoot the shit from time to time. He mentioned that he wanted to run for public office."

"I'll take a wild guess and say you talked him into it."

"I told him Levi Cooke was running unopposed, and that's all I had to say."

"Wait a minute - it's too late to file. This guy's name won't appear on the ballot."

"He's running as a write-in candidate."

"Is he nuts?"

"Somebody needs to run against Levi Cooke. Somebody needs to make that man defend himself," Walter said. "Besides, there's already one too many black candidates in this election. As we both know, black is a popular political flavor these days."

"Everybody in this community loves Levi Cooke, regardless of political party," Ernest said. "Only a fool would run against him on a regular ballot, let alone as a write-in. I bet Cooke wins with 99 percent of the vote."

There had been a challenger, a prominent lawyer who withdrew his candidacy upon his wife's diagnosis with breast cancer. After that, Cooke became the lone candidate.

"Lakehaven has got to be the most apathetic community on the planet when it comes to politics," Ernest said. "Is this Geoffrey Parker making an official announcement or hosting a campaign kickoff?"

"First things first, my friend. He's looking for a campaign office to rent."

Walter left a few minutes later after borrowing ten bucks. As soon as Ernest thought Walter was far enough away from the office, he went out for coffee.

At one time, Sassy Espresso had operated as Babes Coffee Boudoir. The former owner was arrested for running a call girl ring. The shop sat vacant for a while before Parker bought the place and reopened with a new name. The coffee shop hugged an intersection near an upper middle class area of Lakehaven with views of Puget Sound. The breeze rattled the dollhouse shop's white siding and red shingles. On each outside wall of the coffee shop, Sassy Espresso was written in red cursive across a silhouette of an hourglass woman stroking a coffee mug.

Ernest idled in the Jeep, waiting in line to see the busty barista at the drive-thru window - a spicy redhead dressed like a Catholic schoolgirl. With a wink and a shimmy, she charmed an extra dollar out of Ernest.

The back door of Sassy Espresso sprang open, diverting Ernest's attention. A short, double-chinned man in a white shirt and black tie waddled out the door with shiny black shoes clip-clopping across the parking lot toward his Mercedes with a Washington license plate reading "SASSY 1."

Ernest thanked the barista for his coffee and veered around toward the Mercedes, where the pudgy man with slicked-back hair stood silent with a phone to his ear.

"Let me call you back, babe," the man said, stuffing the phone into his pocket. With a ruby ring on his pinky finger, Geoffrey Parker reached out to shake Ernest's hand.

"I hear you're running for state representative against Levi Cooke," Ernest said.

Parker brushed invisible lint from his white shirt. "Walter Wadsworth told me to call you, but things have been hectic lately, as you can probably understand. Business comes first."

"How do you know Walter?"

"He comes by all the time. Very intense guy."

"I know what you mean."

"His column is one of the reasons I'm running for office," Parker said. "Oh, and he speaks highly of you and The Searchlight. He said The Searchlight is the gold standard for newspapers, and he said you're the fairest guy he knows."

"He's an eccentric individual," Ernest said, shrugging. "Gifted, but eccentric."

"Walter is my first official campaign volunteer. He knows a lot about politics, too."

"Good luck with that," Ernest said.

"I hate to be rude, but I'm running late. Maybe you and I can talk a little more in depth about my candidacy later this week."

"Absolutely," Ernest said. "Call anytime."

The Searchlight printed a report about the race:

Sassy Espresso owner and political newcomer Geoffrey Parker has declared his candidacy for state representative as a write-in candidate. Parker, 43, is running against Levi Cooke, the former Seattle Seahawks linebacker and current Christian Castle pastor.

"Voters deserve an alternative, and I'm willing to give it the old college try," Parker told The Searchlight, noting his strategy to attract independent voters. "If elected, I will fight for Lakehaven schools and a more equitable share of state education money. Our children deserve better."

In an obvious advantage, Cooke's recognizable name will appear on the ballot. Cooke is also a first-time candidate. However, according to a recent poll of Lakehaven voters, Parker poses little threat to Cooke's candidacy.

"I know the odds are stacked against me," said Parker, whose red campaign signs have popped up at a handful of Lakehaven intersections. "Every journey begins with a first step. I can't change the education system if I don't try."

No debates have been scheduled for this position.

Cooke told The Searchlight he is willing to debate all the hot-button education issues in a public forum, including the recent accusations that Lakehaven schools discipline a disproportionate number of black students.

"I will fix these atrocious policies in our schools," Cooke said. "The people of Lakehaven are familiar with my commitment to education and public service. As your state representative, I will bring Lakehaven's education and quality of life to the next level."

Cooke has already made an impact in the Lakehaven School District. Earlier this year, he donated $10,000 to buy digital projectors for every classroom at Mount Rainier Elementary School.

Walter found the key

The court allowed Walter to visit Lilly on the third Friday of every month. Visitation was coming up, and Walter wanted to upgrade to a Holiday Inn.

He needed to hustle.

The late afternoon sun cast an orange hue on snow-capped Mount Rainier. Walter gazed at the mountain from the back of a bus, en route to The Searchlight office. He counted his pills and had a dozen left. He kept two and sold the rest before the ride ended.

The bus stopped near The Searchlight. Walter walked past the brick warehouse and across the parking lot toward a nameless office next to an abandoned diner. Inside, Geoffrey Parker attached wooden planks to his red campaign signs that said: "You tried the rest. Now try the best. Parker for Legislature." A small capital letter R in parentheses graced his name like an asterisk.

Walter knocked.

"Come on in," Parker said. He leaned the broom against a wall and wiped his brow. "Lots of work to do here."

"You look busy. I hope this is a good time."

"No problem. I always have time," Parker said. "The single life will do that to you. Do you still want to interview me for

The Searchlight?"

"Of course. I'll work on the column this week," Walter said. "Listen, I need your advice."

"Anything for you, Walter."

"I don't know how else to say it, but I need help," he said, lip quivering. "This divorce has left me short on cash until payday." He sniffled, eyes moped downward. "Today is my daughter's birthday, and I can't even take her out for ice cream. Could you please spare a little?"

"I'm happy to help," said Parker as he reached for his leather wallet, leafed through the bills and tugged on a twenty. "How much do you need?"

"Two hundred dollars."

Parker tucked the bill back into his wallet. "Walter, I - "

"I feel terrible for asking this of you, but I have no other choice."

Parker pulled out all the cash in his wallet - ninety-four dollars, to be exact.

"Tell you what I'm going to do. I'm going to give you this cash as a gift. You don't have to pay me back, but on one condition: you never ask me for money again."

"Thank you. Thank you." Walter bowed his head and gripped the bills. "Anything you need from me, just name it."

"I'm going out to post campaign signs," Parker said. "I could use some help."

"I'm in."

"Great. While you're over on that side of the office, could you grab some pamphlets out of that corner desk?" Parker asked. "I want to hand them out while we're doorbelling."

Walter slid open the gray metal bucket drawer. He grabbed a stack of campaign pamphlets bundled with a rubber band. He snooped in the other drawers and found a single bronze key attached to a red plastic keychain that said "Vote for Parker."

Parker made his way to the door, jangling a bouquet of keys in one hand, holding yard signs under one arm, with a lidded Sassy Espresso coffee mug in his other hand. As Parker fumbled for the main key to lock the door, Walter tucked the spare key in his pocket.

One thing Walter noticed about Parker was an intense need for acceptance.

"What do people think of me?" Parker asked while giving Walter a ride to the library. "What is my reputation in Lakehaven? Just give it to me straight. I can take it. I have a thick skin."

"If you have to ask, you'll never know," Walter said. "The scuttlebutt is that you're the fresh face of change in Lakehaven. There's a buzz, at least in certain circles. Some people think you can shake things up."

"That's good to know," Parker said. "Any word on The Searchlight's endorsement?"

"Let's just say the wind is blowing in your opponent's direction," Walter said. "Sorry to be the bearer of bad news."

Candidates in every Lakehaven election coveted the editorial endorsements, which sometimes made the difference in close races. The race between Parker and Levi Cooke, however, was like a Pinto racing a Ferrari.

"We might not win," Parker said, "but there's no way in hell that Levi Cooke is going unchallenged."

"I admire your courage and integrity," said Walter, fingers brushing across the office key in his front pants pocket.

--

The next afternoon, Walter galloped to Joe Lippy's house with an idea. A groggy-eyed Joe stood in the driveway with a rolled copy of The Searchlight, clad in his robe, pajamas and slippers, puffing his pipe.

"Did you just wake up?" Walter asked. "It's almost 2 p.m."

"Good, you can read a clock," Joe said. "It's chilly out here. Let's go inside."

They walked back to Joe's cave, and Walter sat on a padded stool.

"Would you like some tea?" asked Joe, wiping his nose with the back of his pale veiny hand.

"I'm good," Walter said. "Listen, I know how you can get The Searchlight to endorse you."

"How?"

"I can get them to not endorse anyone. We could level the field. This is an anti-incumbent election so every little bit helps."

"How the hell are you going to stop the endorsement?" Joe said, waving his hands with fury while shooing a fly away. "At this point, I'll try anything. I would try to bribe the paper, you see, but I'm damn near out of money." He paused and raised an eyebrow in Walter's direction.

Walter swallowed.

"Listen, I have a favor to ask. I have visitation with Lilly next week," he said, sensing the hostility from Joe. "You and I both know that a clean hotel room and a continental breakfast is more appropriate for my little girl than the Shady Acres Motel. I realize this isn't the best time to ask, but I've exhausted every option. Can you help me? Please? It's one of our last visits before she moves to Spokane with her mother."

Joe knew when he opened the door that Walter would ask for money. He dug out three twenties, a ten, two fives and eight singles from his billfold on the counter.

"Here, just take what I got," Joe said, shoving the bills into Walter's hands while he exhaled smoke. "Take the whole damn wad."

"Thank you," said Walter, bowing his head. "You're a true friend."

"I'll put it on your tab."

Walter had one-hundred and thirty-eight dollars in his pocket. A room with two beds at the Holiday Inn cost ninety-eight bucks a night. That left him with forty dollars, and of course, he had to take Lilly out for pizza.

In the meantime, Walter walked back to Parker's campaign office, where the lights were out. He helped himself to the mini-refrigerator. He cracked opened a Pepsi and washed down a pill. Three takeout containers from Ming Dynasty called like the Sirens. Skipping the chopsticks, he scarfed down the cold beef and broccoli, his fingers sticky with brown sauce. He smacked his lips, chewed with his mouth open and finished with a belch. He washed his hands and face in the spotless bathroom sink before plopping down on the campaign couch, where he fell asleep, embedding his body odor on the cushions. The white hat covered his face.

Walter left before sunrise and locked the office door behind him.

The endorsement

The familiar footsteps crescendoed into Ernest's office. On the desk, Walter laid down a king-sized skunk-scented joint.

"Dude! What's this for?" Ernest said, smothering the doobie with that day's newspaper.

"It's my way of saying thank you for helping me become a better writer," Walter said. "Smells like some good shit."

"What's the catch?"

"No catch. A friend gave it to me. I don't like weed. Makes me too tired and slow," Walter said. "I figured that you, being a raging liberal media maven, would appreciate it."

They laughed.

"How's my book coming?" Walter asked, his fingers steepled. "Tell me some good news."

"Almost done," Ernest said. "Sorry about the delay. I've been swamped this week with breaking news."

"Let me talk to your publisher. I'll tell him that you need more time to work on my book."

"I worked on it all day Sunday," said Ernest, red-faced. "Quit nagging me about it. I have a newspaper to run."

"We're sitting on a golden goose, my friend."

"True. The people who read your columns are hardcore," said Ernest, stroking his chin. "They'll eat this up. I bet we could sell a couple thousand copies. Publishers will beg to take it nationwide. Cha-ching!"

Walter listened with wide eyes and straight posture. He had mastered his audience. Walter was convinced that he could get Oprah Winfrey to discuss the book on her show and make him an instant millionaire. Ernest gave up on telling him otherwise.

One option for an investor, they agreed, was Theodore Rosewater, who owned most of Lakehaven.

"I'll set up an appointment with Money Bags," Walter said, referring to Rosewater. "On a different subject, I wanted to call something to your attention. I'm concerned about the newspaper's endorsement."

"For which race?"

"School board. You need to endorse Joe Lippy. You'll look like a fool if you support Ted Farley and the status quo. The Searchlight will lose all respect."

"How the hell do you know?"

"Trust me. I've followed campaigns since the days when you were in diapers," Walter said. "If you endorse, you lose."

"You're crazy. We pick somebody for every race."

"If you endorse, you lose," Walter said. "You give people a reason to hate you. At least with no endorsement, no one gets hurt. I know you don't want to hurt anyone."

"Let me worry about the endorsement," said Ernest, putting on his glasses. "I need to get back to work. Call me about the meeting with Rosewater."

--

In an aerial photo, Lakehaven resembled a lopsided concrete doughnut, criss-crossed with asphalt arteries. The green hole in the doughnut was Rosewater's urban evergreen sanctuary. This third-generation housing developer's family had built homes since Lakehaven's log cabin days. Rosewater also loved Walter's columns.

Walter arrived early at the Rosewater mansion and was greeted at the door by Money Bags himself. Rosewater had grown up privileged. He dined while the commoners ate, and he summered while the rest vacationed.

They settled in the library in two Victorian-era chairs, and the butler set a tray of tea cups on the table between them.

"The book is more of an independent venture," Walter said. "I'm trying to clear a few hurdles."

"You need an angel investor," Rosewater said.

"Three-thousand copies is the magic number to catch a major publisher's attention," Walter said, noticing a stray bread crumb on Rosewater's wool sweater. Walter leaned forward and lowered his voice, nearly to a whisper: "Mr. Rosewater, what we need is an angel."

The meeting ended with a handshake and Rosewater's encouragement to meet when the proofs for the book arrived. "Please call me anytime."

Walter called Rosewater later that week, after the mom-and-pop printer in Olympia sent two sample copies to The Searchlight office. The book was plain white with black lettering on the cover and binding: "Telling it like it is: Lakehaven's education crisis." Inside was every school board speech and Searchlight essay he had written so far, which made for a quick read. Walter noted that each entry in the book was perfect for reading sessions on the toilet.

Rosewater invited Walter over for tea in his backyard bonsai garden overlooking Puget Sound and the sunset. The local aristocrat put on his thin-framed spectacles and leafed through the paperback book.

"I loved this one," said Rosewater, holding open the book to the first column Walter wrote for The Searchlight.

Walter left Rosewater's haven with a check for five-hundred dollars. He sought refuge at the bus station as the hailstorm pelted the concrete with bouncing ice bullets. He peeled off the soaking wet baseball cap, wrung out the rainwater, and put it back on.

--

Walter's lips whistled as he inhaled the crisp morning air and stepped off the bus. He felt refreshed after a good night's sleep at the Shady Acres Motel. The bus departed, belching a trail of exhaust fumes as the overcast skies resumed their drizzle.

Walter and his white sneakers splashed toward the road. He crossed in the middle of traffic, half a block from the crosswalk. A scraggly veteran in a bumper-stickered Ford truck squealed to a stop. He honked at Walter, shook a fist, spun his tires and left the scene.

Walter paused in the median, where he trampled the damp shredded woodchip mulch. The median was a landscaped oasis that split the asphalt artery in two directions.

The Searchlight building was in sight, like a beacon, one wet block away.

Walter and his cramping shins wheeled their way into Ernest Handsy's newspaper-saturated office.

"I just got off the phone with a reader who loves your column," said Ernest, leaning forward in a leather chair. He hesitated to connect anyone with Walter. "She's a retired teacher."

"I need to get in touch with this woman."

"She didn't leave a number," said Ernest, rubbing his throbbing forehead. "Also got a call from a woman who said you're a lying pig."

"Let me guess - she didn't leave her number, either."

"She hung up before I could ask how she really felt."

Walter smirked before snapping into business mode. "Listen, this is off the subject, but I have an idea and I need your help."

"We already typed up your column for this week."

"No, this involves an urgent matter. I need a ride to the pharmacy. However, I'm ten dollars short for my prescription. Because I like you, and because you sacrifice your time to help with the column, I'll give you four painkillers for ten bucks and a ride."

"Vicodins?" Ernest asked, eyebrows raised.

"Oxioids."

"Those are serious. I'm not sure I want to mess with those."

"You'll be fine. Smooth sailing. They're usually five bucks each. I'll give you four for ten."

"Man, all right," Ernest said, fidgeting his clenched hands, blood pressure spiking. "My meeting isn't until two o'clock. You ready now?"

Thirty minutes later, Walter dropped four white discs, each stamped with a number fifteen, into Ernest's open palm. Ernest drove him to Mount Rainier Elementary School for a spur-of-the-moment visit, one of the last before Lilly moved to Spokane with her mother.

"See you tomorrow," Walter said, shutting the Jeep door behind him, heading toward the school's front doors. Ernest cupped and jangled the pills before zipping them into the front pocket of his rain jacket. On the way back to the office, Ernest steered through Sassy Espresso.

"Hey there, big guy," said the young blonde in a ponytail, a white cowgirl hat and bikini-coated bosom. "Do you want your usual four-shot mocha?"

Ernest froze in his seat as she poured the espresso, licked her red lips and swayed her round hips.

"You want whipped cream on that, big guy?"

He mumbled and tipped her three dollars.

Even strong coffee couldn't cure Ernest's jackhammer headache, which he had blamed on caffeine withdrawal and Walter. Damn editorial board meeting. He needed relief. The aspirin bottle was empty. Back in the office, Ernest pulled a pill from his jacket pocket, pinched it between thumb and forefinger, and squinted at the number fifteen.

Five minutes until the board meeting, which should last no more than thirty minutes, he thought. He devoured a half-eaten salami hoagie, swallowed the pill with coffee and barreled toward the conference room. Ernest took his seat next to the publisher, who sniffled with a sinus infection.

"Let's make this meeting as brief as possible," the publisher said, wiping his nose with a hanky. "Last week, we agreed unanimously on the school district levy. Ernest's editorial really hit it on the head. Thank you, everyone, for your input."

The board's six faces turned toward Ernest and smiled as the publisher continued with the meeting agenda. Ernest felt the pill's magic as it mushed his attention span like a rotted pumpkin.

"This week, we're picking the candidate for the Lakehaven School Board."

"That's a no-brainer," piped up one board member. "If this board endorses Joe Lippy, I'm quitting on the spot."

"What a yo-yo," said another board member.

"He drives me nuts."

"He always says the same old thing, over and over and over again."

The publisher cleared his throat.

"I suppose that settles it, then. The only opinion we haven't heard from is Ernest."

The six faces turned toward Ernest and smiled again. Ernest's mouth hung open as he stared at a map of Lakehaven on the far wall.

"Ernest?" the publisher said, waving to get his attention.

"Huh?"

"Are we unanimous?"

"Unanimous? About what?"

The board guffawed in unison as the zonked editor played it off.

"Endorsing Ted Farley over Joe Lippy is the practical choice," Ernest said, more composed.

"Well then, that settles it," the publisher said. "Ernest, I want that endorsement on my desk by the end of the week."

As the room cleared, the publisher pulled Ernest aside and whispered.

"Are you all right? You look like a goddamn zombie."

"Exhausted, yes. I'm very exhausted," Ernest said. "I was trying to last until the meeting was over. Mind if I take the rest of the day off?"

"For crying out loud, get some sleep," the publisher said, looking Ernest up and down. "See you in the morning, ready to work."

While Ernest drowsed through the meeting, Walter signed in at Mount Rainier Elementary for a visitor's pass. The secretaries grimaced in unison as soon as Walter walked away. Lilly's classroom was at the end of the hall. The classroom was dark and locked, and he assumed Lilly was at lunch. He felt the noise and vibrations of a crowd in the cafeteria on the other end of the school. Like a bowling ball to the head, the pills were stronger than he expected, and Walter's reality oozed like the slime trail of a slug. He leaned into a white porcelain water fountain to wet his dry mouth. He ducked into a somewhat secluded bathroom, fumbled with the lock on the stall door, and sat on the toilet with his knees tucked and heels on the lid, and a fist supporting his forehead like an ode to The Thinker statue. He nodded off, tranced and relieved.

Walter awoke to the contrasting voices of a man and a boy echoing in the secluded bathroom. Walter swayed his loaded head toward the door and eyed the tile floor. Two pairs of feet, facing each other. Two little sneakers and two big sneakers.

"I talked to your family's doctor, and he is requiring me, by law, to give you a brief physical," said a man's voice. "I need to make sure you are healthy."

"Um, Mr. Hudson, I want to go back to gym class."

"Just hold still, please. Are you still my special boy?"

"Um, Mr. Hudson," said the boy. "I don't like this."

The tremble in the boy's voice sent a jolt through Walter, who leaped off the toilet and busted down the stall door with anger exploding like a pressure cooker packed with TNT.

"What the - " said Mr. Hudson as Walter shoved him head-first into the concrete wall. Walter grabbed the boy by the shoulders and told him to run. The boy pulled up his underwear and pants as he escaped.

Mr. Hudson, in his red running suit, stumbled toward the bathroom door as it swung closed. Walter snatched the red collar and yanked backward, smacking the gym teacher's head on the tile floor like stone on stone.

"You fucking piece of shit!" Walter yelled. He raised his leg chest high and stomped Mr. Hudson's face. Blood splattered on the white walls, white sinks, white stall doors, white sneakers, white headband and the white stripes on the red running suit. The man vomited blood and spat out white teeth with flesh-tipped roots. He groaned and rolled. Walter limped out of the bathroom, bloody footprints leading around the corner and out the back doors. With a visitor's pass clipped to his jacket collar, he caught a bus down the street.

Lilly came home after school and said Mr. Hudson was attacked in the bathroom. Rose listened in shock. The Searchlight reported the incident in the next day's newspaper:

A gym teacher was rushed to the hospital after a brutal assault Thursday at Mount Rainier Elementary School.

Lance Hudson, who teaches physical education and works as a counselor, was attacked by an unknown assailant during his lunch break around 11:30 a.m.

The assault occurred in a bathroom at the school. According to police, the teacher suffered a concussion, a broken nose and face lacerations. As of press time, he was listed in serious condition.

Lakehaven police are searching for suspects and witnesses. Anyone with information is asked to call 911.

Hudson is a popular figure at Mount Rainier Elementary. He regularly emcees student events and volunteers as an after-school counselor for at-risk youth.

Superintendent Harvey Oakes issued a statement to The Searchlight.

"I am shocked and saddened by the tragic events of today. The safety of students and staff has always been and will always be our top priority. It is my hope that police will find justice for Mr. Hudson," Oakes said. "Mr. Hudson is a role model and a hero for many of our children. He is in our hearts, thoughts and prayers."

Campaign volunteer

Geoffrey Parker and Walter met for lunch at Sub King, the grilled onion oasis of Lakehaven. Parker ordered the spicy cheesesteak, and the cook went right to work, slapping and chopping the sizzling meat with twin spatulas across the scorched metal surface. Walter ordered a meatball sub on wheat bread, Parker paid for both meals, and they claimed a corner booth with a fresh-wiped table.

"I'm fairly confident about the campaign so far," Parker said, wiping his mouth with a wadded napkin. "I've knocked on more than three-thousand doors. I wave signs downtown every morning, and I'm getting a lot of honks from drivers."

"This write-in campaign just might work," Walter said. "I can just picture the front-page headline now."

"An endorsement from The Searchlight's editorial board would help," Parker said, brushing dandruff off his shoulder. "Have you heard anything?"

"They're endorsing the other guy."

"Damn, that's what I thought. How do we change their minds?"

"They go with the status quo. Always have, always will. They are afraid to vote for change, which is what you represent for Lakehaven."

"I agree. The people of Lakehaven need a boots-on-the-ground leader. Why does the community have to go before the school board or city council to be heard? I will be a phone call away. That's all on the record, by the way, in case you're still writing an article about me."

"If we can't get them to endorse you," Walter said, "maybe we can void their endorsement."

"That's impossible. The paper picks the winner in just about every election."

"Trust me, it can be done," Walter said, sinking his new teeth into the meatball sandwich.

After scoring more pills on a dreary late-night bus, Walter arrived at Parker's dark campaign office near bedtime, snickering at the red Vote for Parker sign in the window. He fumbled for his borrowed key.

He opened the door and locked eyes with Parker and a barely legal barista who were both naked. They all gasped in unison.

"How in the hell did you get a key?" said Parker as he stumbled around to the back of the couch and crouched, clad only in black knee-high socks and a gold watch. The barista snatched a blanket.

"Listen, I must have picked it up by mistake," Walter said from the opposite end of the office. "Let's discuss the plan another time."

"Get the hell out of here!" Parker screamed, baring his teeth and pointing at the door.

"Listen, Geoff, I can - "

"Go! Get out!" Parker threw a shoe that barely missed Walter's head. "Get the hell out of here! Go! Go!"

Walter backed out the door and booked across the street for the next bus to downtown Seattle. The bus rolled past the hospital where Mr. Hudson the gym teacher slept these days. Medical scaffolding stabilized Mr. Hudson's head and neck.

The once active teacher in the red running suit with white stripes was now bedridden in a checkered hospital gown.

A flat-screen TV the size of a suitcase was mounted in the ceiling corner of Mr. Hudson's hospital room. Numbed and drugged, Mr. Hudson watched the show "Town Talk." His black-and-blue eyes widened at the grainy interview between Guy Petty and a familiar black man in a pinstripe suit.

Mr. Hudson pressed the volume button on the remote control with his thumb. Walter's words on the previously taped show filled the hospital room:

> "Education is a sum of its parts. Teachers can only do so much. God bless them. They don't just educate our kids. They raise our kids. They toil away, day after day, with no resources, and all because the politicians in Olympia refuse to do what's right. When the teachers suffer, so do the children."

It's a lie

Parker had fallen into Walter's whirlpool of sin. On top of that, Walter harassed the baristas at Sassy Espresso to the point where three top earners quit in disgust.

"He's the creepiest customer in history," said one blonde beauty, whose smile and curves had customers lining up before sunrise.

It's all business, thought Parker, who requested a meeting with The Searchlight editor.

"He stole the keys to my office," Parker said, hands on his head. "He was sleeping in my campaign office, for Christ's sake. Now I know why my couch smells like an armpit."

"How long was he staying there?"

"Who knows?"

"What else was he doing there?" Ernest asked. "I heard he was into some weird shit."

"Who knows?" said Parker, throwing his arms up. "When I confronted him about the keys, he denied everything. The next day, the keys are in the desk. Explain that."

"Did he steal anything?"

"He ate my leftover Chinese food and drank all my sodas," Parker said. "Man, he is too much."

"I've said it before, and I'll say it again," Ernest said.

"There's no such thing as a little bit of Walter."

"Looks like we both have a deadly case of Walter."

They revealed how, in an effort to avoid Walter, they spent more time outside meeting people and such. Parker had gone into campaign overdrive by waving signs and knocking on doors all day long. Ernest had joined the Lakehaven Rotary Club and helped organize a project to plant trees at Lakehaven High School.

"I do want to call a more serious matter to your attention," Parker said, tweaking the knot on his tie. "Did you know that he 'borrowed' money from Levi Cooke?"

"What do you want me to do about it?" Ernest asked, taking off his glasses.

"I respect you and The Searchlight. That's why I wanted to tell you before you heard it through the rumor mill," Parker said. "I feel it's best to be upfront with you. This is a pre-emptive strike, so to speak."

"What the hell are you getting at? If you think you can spin me, you're wrong," Ernest said. "Don't you dare poison this newspaper."

"We're cutting off ties with Walter," Parker said. "We just want him to leave us alone."

"Why are you telling me?"

"There's so much you don't know about this guy who appears in your newspaper once a week," Parker said. "Do you remember reading about a guy who was arrested at the Paragon pool showers? It was in your paper."

Ernest nodded.

"Maybe you should do some more digging on that incident. Use your journalistic skills and resources," said Parker, standing up to leave. "Good luck."

Ernest realized what Parker was talking about and had no plans to tell his bosses. He wanted to cut the newspaper's cord with Walter and look like the hero, rather than sink on

Walter's ship. The publisher had warned Ernest about his prize columnist's troublemaking after a particularly venomous call from a massage parlor madam.

"If I hear one more thing about Walter," the publisher told the editor, "he's gone."

On the way out of the office, Parker handed an envelope to the receptionist. The envelope was addressed to "Searchlight Publisher." Inside the envelope was the police report from Walter's hotel shower arrest.

--

The next morning, Ernest arrived at the office before sunrise. He wanted plenty of time to prepare himself for firing Walter.

Technically, it was a termination of Walter's freelance contract. Whatever you called it, The Searchlight publishers no longer wanted Walter in the paper.

Ernest drank lukewarm coffee and glanced at his watch every fifteen seconds. He soon heard Walter's footsteps grow louder until they stopped at his doorway.

"Big Ernest, how are you today?" Walter sat in the leather chair, satchel on his lap. He leaned over, put two fingers on the door's edge and swung it shut.

"Listen," Ernest said. "This isn't easy to say, so I'll just say it. The Searchlight no longer needs your services."

Walter's eyes widened and his mouth fell open. A few seconds of silence followed.

"Walter, we know about the arrest at the hotel, and we know about your scheme to sabotage the election endorsements."

"It's a lie."

"Walter, this reflects poorly on the newspaper."

"It's a lie. Where did you hear that?"

"Doesn't matter where we heard it. We can't run your column anymore."

"What?"

"We're dropping your column. It's done. Kaput."

Walter exhaled. "Aren't you going to go to bat for me? After all I've done for this paper?"

"Go to bat for you? Do you know how many times I've covered for your ass?" said Ernest, rising out of his chair, trembling. "You're done. Now get the hell out of here."

Walter picked up his satchel and left the editor's office. He walked past the news team, through the advertising department, around the receptionist and out the door. He caught a bus to Seattle and sprawled across two empty seats in the back. A frumpy woman in her mid-fifties was sitting across from him and smiled, awkwardly, like a long lost aunt.

Walter smiled.

"Do you write for The Searchlight? Are you Walter Wadsworth?"

He nodded.

"Oh, I knew it was you," she said, clasping her hands in joy. "I love your column. You have such a big heart. Thank you for telling it like it is."

"You're welcome, ma'am," Walter said, leaning his head against the frigid bus window.

"I loved the one you wrote about your daughter," she said. "I had tears in my eyes after reading it. You made me want to hug my children and my precious little grandbabies."

"That's great, ma'am," Walter said. "Listen, I don't mean to be rude, but I've had a long day and would like to rest for a minute."

"Oh, I'm sorry. Don't mind me," she said. "I'm just excited to meet you in person."

Back at The Searchlight, the publisher busted Ernest's balls for being late to the editorial board meeting.

"Nice of you to join us," the publisher sneered as Ernest slid into a chair. The editorial board met at 9 a.m. Thursdays in the windowless, lifeless, chilly conference room. A dozen tall-backed leather chairs lined a long maple table.

The board consisted of The Searchlight's publisher, editor, managing editor and four community volunteers. This year's lineup included a retired lawyer, a retired teacher, a retired businessman and a retired politician. The publisher planned to retire next year. Ernest felt destined to work there for life.

The topic of today's meeting was the election endorsements for the Lakehaven School Board. The editorial board voted unanimously for Ted Farley over Joe Lippy.

Ernest wrote the editorial for Saturday's opinion page:

> The Searchlight editorial board unanimously endorses Ted Farley for Lakehaven School Board. Farley has earned a second term on the board for his efforts to engage the community on education.
>
> In the past four years, Farley has lobbied the Legislature on behalf of Lakehaven education interests. He hosts monthly community forums with a question-and-answer session. His annual Feed the Kiddos Food Drive has provided after-school meals to hundreds of children from low-income households.
>
> Last week, the Lakehaven Rotary Club honored Farley as Educator of the Decade, and established the Farley Scholarship for $500, given annually to a student who demonstrates outstanding public service.
>
> Farley's opponent, Joe Lippy, has some eccentric ideas for reforming education in Lakehaven. The editorial board believes Lippy will not play well with other members of the board. Lippy is not a team player, and his tendency to go against the grain will hurt students in the long run. He shuns conformity for the sake of shunning conformity.

Only a united team effort, with everyone riding the same bus, will lead our children to success.

The Searchlight recommends that voters go with depth. Farley is the best fit for Lakehaven schools.

The editorial board unanimously endorsed Levi Cooke for the state House of Representatives, representing Lakehaven's legislative district:

In the November general election, The Searchlight endorses Levi Cooke (D) for state representative.

Cooke offers the right mix of financial know-how and vision for the future of Lakehaven and Washington. He has demonstrated a commitment to this community, particularly in education. Cooke led the construction of a church that attracts thousands of people who breathe life into the local economy. The church also serves as a social and cultural hub. He has donated thousands of dollars to local charities and Lakehaven schools, most notably a batch of digital projectors at Mount Rainier Elementary School. Cooke creates opportunities for others by setting goals and achieving them. That's the type of representation Lakehaven needs.

His opponent, Sassy Espresso owner Geoffrey Parker (R), is running as a write-in candidate. Parker lacks a record of public achievement sufficient enough to top Cooke. Despite his success as a small business owner, Parker has failed to present a strong case for how he could make Lakehaven a better place to live, work and play. That said, the Searchlight's editorial board applauds Parker for running a clean campaign.

In this election, and in these times, Lakehaven needs a state representative who presents a vision and backs it with a plan of action. The people need a leader who takes charge instead of looking for the person in charge. Cooke has vowed to secure more state money for Lakehaven's schools. After proving his mettle at the local level, this promise seems realistic at the state level.

Cooke brings value to Lakehaven's quality of life, and this district is lucky to have him. He earns a solid endorsement from The Searchlight.

You want happy ending?

Walter's political partners were slaughtered at the polls. Early election results showed Levi Cooke leading Geoffrey Parker with 98 percent of the vote, and Ted Farley leading Joe Lippy with 73 percent.

On election night, as the candidates crowded around televisions for the first results, Walter was on a bus to Seattle. He exited on Aurora Avenue, right in front of the Siesta Motel. He booked a room, popped a pill and jaywalked across the road to Minh's Massage Parlor.

The letters on the parlor's sign glowed with a soft red hue, bright enough for Walter to see the time on his watch. A tiny bell jingled on the door as he entered the red-light den, which smelled like baby powder and tea tree oil.

An older Asian madam in a red pantsuit greeted him and collected the entry fee. "Welcome," she said, reaching for Walter's hand and leading him through the foyer, down a short hallway and into the lounge. Fluorescent lights illuminated the room. Red velvet cushioned benches lined the walls and music pulsed in the corner speakers.

"Pick one you like," the madame asked, gesturing in a sweeping motion. "They are all beautiful." A dozen Asian women lined up across the middle of the lounge, each one cracking a Mona Lisa smile and batting brush-length eye-lashes.

He assumed the women were of legal age. These parlors had ties to organized crime and sex trafficking.

Walter patted the wad of cash in his front pocket and nodded toward a woman in a red cocktail dress. The five-foot-tall honey had a young face and grapefruit tits. She took him by the arm.

The music from the lounge dimmed as they walked down another hall to the last room on the left. The room was clean and smelled like vanilla incense. Next to the burning fragrance on the nightstand was a brass lamp with a low-watt bulb. The massage table, draped in hospital-white sheets, looked more like a portable bed. Framed photos of flowers and landscapes graced the otherwise bare lavender walls.

"I'll be right back. You get undressed," the masseuse said.

Walter disrobed and assumed the position. The lamp cast his shadow on one wall, like a skyline of rolling hills. He watched his shadow and shifted to get comfortable.

The masseuse returned with another towel and a bottle of massage oil.

"You relax, OK?" she said. "I make you feel good."

The massage was decent, he thought. He felt pampered. The masseuse straddled his back and dug in with her fingertips and elbows. She walked her fingers up and down his spine and rubbed tea tree oil all over his bony back. She karate-chopped his shoulder blades and trapezius muscles with both hands in a drum roll rhythm. She told him to roll over on his back so that she could massage his front.

"You want happy ending?" she asked, leaning forward with cherry-red lips, breathing in his face.

"Yes."

--

On the other side of Lakehaven's tracks, Rose and Grandma chatted at the kitchen table over two fat mugs of hot coffee. Rose filled one-third of the cup with cream. Grandma drank it black.

"Whew, that's strong stuff," Rose said after the first sip.

"Your father liked strong coffee," Grandma said. "I like coffee so strong that it jumps into my cup when I whistle for it."

Boxes of dishes and cookware were piled in the kitchen. In the living room were more stacks of boxes packed to the brim. In the bare kitchen, Rose picked the hardened white glaze off a half-eaten cinnamon roll on a saucer. Grandma spread The Searchlight across the table.

"Let's see what kind of hot air that Mr. Wonderful is blowing this week," Grandma said, scanning the pages for Walter's mug shot. "Looks like they didn't print him this week. I'm pleasantly surprised."

"Really? You mean I can actually read the Saturday newspaper without wanting to vomit?"

They laughed. Rose reached for the coffee pot and topped off their mugs.

"Once you're in Spokane, you won't have to read his drivel or see that shit-eating grin on his face," Grandma said.

"Yes. Even Lilly's school isn't safe, considering what happened to her poor gym teacher, Mr. Hudson."

"Oh, that poor man," Grandma said. "I never heard if they caught the psycho who nearly killed him."

"Last I heard, police had no suspects," Rose said. "That's one more reason why we need to get the hell out of Lakehaven. Too many nutcases running around."

"What does Lilly think about moving to Spokane? She's never even been there."

"She's worried about going to a new school and leaving her friends behind, that kind of thing," Rose said.

Grandma folded the broadsheet newspaper to its original shape and slid it across the table. "What about Walter?"

"What about him?"

"How does she feel about moving and not seeing her father as much?"

"She understands," Rose said. "I told her not to get her hopes up. I explained what her father was really like."

When a killer becomes a hero

Walter peeped inside his ex-wife's house every so often. This time he saw the moving boxes, stacked in threes. Framed artwork leaned against the now bare walls.

He gazed at the fireplace's reflection through the picture window. His breath fogged the glass as he pulled the cuffs of his goose-down coat over numb gloveless fists. He crouched behind a shrub.

The fireplace popped and crackled inside the house, shaking Rose away from her novel with a gasp and wide eyes. She shrugged, reclined in her La-Z-Boy chair and continued reading.

"That's my chair," Walter whispered to himself. He squatted and watched some more. His nose was runny. His muscles ached. His eyes watered.

Sitting across from Rose, with feet also reclined, was Grandma, reading The Searchlight. She turned the pages beneath a lamp as the fireplace warmed her stocking feet.

Lilly sat with legs crossed, five feet from the TV, combing the hair of a Barbie doll.

He was so caught up in the show that Walter failed to notice a police car paused in its tracks, right in front of the house. The officer shined a flashlight toward the bushes.

Walter held his breath and stood still, shielded by shrubs. The cop drove away.

Walter exhaled and cut through an alley toward the bus station. He had one pill left.

His dealer was staying in the Wishing Well Motel, two blocks from the bus station and adjacent to the Shady Acres Motel. Walter knocked three times on the door of room two.

"What the fuck do you want?" said a man from the other side of the door.

"I'm looking for Mrs. O," Walter said.

"I don't know no Mrs. O. Now get the fuck out of here."

"It's Walter. C'mon, open up."

The man behind the door unlocked the deadbolt and cracked the door wide enough to peek, then unchained the door.

"Walter, my brother, come in, come in," said the dealer, scanning the parking lot before locking and chaining the door. "Just covering my ass, know what I'm saying?"

"Of course," Walter said.

"Right on, right on," the dealer said, jittery and talking fast. "Let's see it."

Walter opened his brown satchel and pulled out a jumbo plastic bag of neon green nuggets twinkling with pearly white trichomes.

"Mmm, mmm, mmm!" the dealer said, holding a bud to his nostrils. "This is some stinky-ass weed. You need to start putting this shit in mason jars, brother. The pigs will smell it a mile away."

The dealer disappeared to the bathroom for a moment and returned with an orange bottle of Oxioids. The bottle contained one hundred pills.

"Brother, I keep it real with you, you know that," the dealer said. "You keep bringing the weed, and I'll keep bringing the meds. Know what I'm saying?

Walter nodded, ate a pill and headed for the bus station, ready to call it a night.

--

After The Searchlight canceled Walter's column, he schmoozed with the editor at the Seattle Daily News. Their deal was one column a month, on the first Monday. It wasn't a prime weekly slot like at The Searchlight, nor was he paid, but at least he could make contacts.

In other new partnerships, Candy typed with proficiency on a laptop computer. She sat with legs folded on the motel bed as Walter paced the room with the tension of a sermon. Incidentally, Walter was later glad that the following essay never made it into the book he produced with Ernest, but only because he felt it set a bad example for his daughter.

> When a killer becomes a hero
> By Walter Wadsworth, guest columnist
>
> A killer has earned my respect.
> Earlier this month, a child molester was murdered at the state prison in Walla Walla. The man, whose name I will not dignify in print, was found guilty of kidnapping and raping a 13-year-old boy. The boy had been tied to a tree in the woods and left to die.
> Just six months before his release, the molester met his maker. A new cellmate strangled him with a shoelace. The cellmate, who had been abused by his uncle throughout childhood, was already serving twenty years for armed robbery. He will spend the rest of his life behind bars.
> I want to shake that cellmate's hand. I want to thank him for his positive contribution to society. One less sexual predator means at least one less child is harmed.

That cellmate is a hero.

I am a father of a little girl. I will give my life to protect her life. And if you are a parent, please know that I am willing to say what you silently think when it comes to punishing these sick perverts who harm our children.

The U.S. penitentiary system is filled with murderers, robbers, gangsters and violent career criminals who live by their own code. This prison hierarchy ranks child molesters as the ultimate scum. The average "chomo" is housed in protective custody, separated from inmates who would love to bash in their skulls and stab their guts out.

Considering the relatively light sentences that child molesters receive, the inmates perform a public service by picking up where the courts leave off.

Child molesters are fully aware of the fate that awaits them in prison. I once saw a news report about a child molester who jumped to his death from the eighth floor of the courthouse balcony. He had faced a sentence of six years for repeatedly molesting a young girl at his church.

The news of his death put a smile on my face. Finally, justice was served.

Why aren't the legal penalties more severe for adults who molest children? Unfortunately, that would create higher stakes and potentially put more young lives in jeopardy. It's a wicked paradox. If the penalty for raping a child were death, then child molesters would have more incentive to kill their victims.

As a father, I find comfort in knowing that monsters who hurt children will face hell in prison. Such crimes against children are akin to murdering their souls.

I want to extend my deepest gratitude to all the murderers, robbers, thieves, gang leaders and any other prisoners who have made child molesters pay for their crimes. When it comes to justice for our children, every bit helps.

The Seattle paper was too big, too secure, too corporate to let Walter attach himself like a barnacle the way he did in Lakehaven. It didn't take long before his luck dried up. While wasted on pills, he puked on the editor's desk while meeting about his second column. The Seattle Daily News shut the door forever.

Walter's contacts in Lakehaven had also dried up. He laid low, stricken with paranoia whenever a police cruiser passed, unaware that the case had turned in his favor.

And from the morphine-friendly confines of a hospital bed, Mr. Hudson described his attacker as a black man in a suit. He had trouble recalling details from the incident due to brain trauma. In fact, Walter had worn jeans and sneakers that day, and disposed of the bloody clothing in a trash can at the bus station.

No staff at the school recalled seeing a black man in a suit.

"The only black man who came in that day was Walter Wadsworth, and he wasn't wearing any suit, I can tell you that much," the school secretary told a police detective. "I don't remember what he was wearing, but he smelled like a bum."

A newly sober Walter

Walter had shuddered when learning that Rose accepted a job in Spokane, almost three-hundred miles away. The law required her to live within the state, and they moved as far from Walter as they could. Walter's first visitation weekend, as allowed by the courts, was spent at a Holiday Inn near the elementary school, where Rose taught. The hotel room drained all his cash. Withdrawal symptoms gnawed at his body. He chose the hotel over pills.

Every muscle ached and his abdomen cramped without mercy. Sweat soaked the clothes on his gaunt frame.

"Daddy, why are your hands shaking?" Lilly asked as Walter came out of the bathroom. "Daddy, why are you so sweaty? Are you OK? Daddy?"

"Baby girl, I'm fine," he said, grimacing. "I ate some bad fish."

"What kind of fish?"

"I don't know," Walter said. "I'll be right back."

Walter wretched a mix of water and bile into the toilet. This time he heaved hard enough to defecate.

"Sweetheart," said Walter, the room spinning. "I'm sorry. You need to go home. Daddy feels sick."

"Daddy, I want to take care of you!"

"Lilly, I'm sorry."

A hunched-over Walter opened the taxi door and gave Rose's address. Walter wiped his runny nose and tossed the driver his last twenty dollars. Lilly sobbed.

"Sweetheart, I am so sorry. Daddy is feeling really sick. I don't want you to catch what I got."

"I thought you ate bad fish. Are you going to be OK?"

"Daddy's fine. I'll be fine."

"I'm worried."

"I promise we'll do this right next time. You and me and me and you." He overcame the shakes for a moment and poked Lilly's little belly. She giggled. It brought a kernel of peace to the situation.

"OK, Daddy. I love you. Please be careful."

"I love you, sweetheart. I'll see you soon, I promise." He barely had the strength to wave.

--

When the taxi brought Lilly home, Rose freaked out and called the cops. She grilled Lilly on Walter's behavior and concluded that he was "high on drugs." She knew he had a heroin problem years ago, and assumed he was back on the smack, which was what she told the police.

While the cops searched for Walter at the hotel, their culprit trekked to a rest stop near the interstate to hustle for pills. En route to the restroom, he passed the information booth, which was manned by an elderly couple who served coffee to the homeless people who parked overnight.

Walter stumbled into the men's room and gagged on the stench of piss and cigarettes. He entered the last stall and locked the door. A few minutes later, a mystery man in blue jeans and muddy boots walked into the adjacent stall. In the metal wall separating the two stalls was a round gash with the words "glory hole" above the opening. The man in the next stall poked his finger through the glory hole and gave the "come here" signal. Walter tapped the finger and said the price was twenty dollars.

The man in the next stall slipped a twenty dollar bill through the hole. Seconds after Walter snatched the bill, the man in the next stall inserted his erect penis through the glory hole. Walter wiped a tear from his cheek, took a breath, closed his eyes and allowed a recent massage parlor tryst to take over his thoughts.

After the deed was done, Walter asked the man behind the hole for Oxioids. The man poked two fingers through the glory hole, snatched the twenty, and shoved a pill into Walter's palm. Walter checked for authenticity, dry-swallowed the drug and bolted out the door.

Walter still needed cash for the ride back to the wet side of the mountains. He ripped a piece of cardboard from a box in a convenience store dumpster, and with a black pen from his satchel, scrawled "Homeless and hungry. Anything helps. God bless." He stood at the freeway off-ramp, held the chicken-scratched sign to his chest, and lowered his head. Drivers in the Audis and BMWs and Porsches stared straight ahead and ignored him. His first score came from a family of three who were crowded in the front bench seat of a rusty Datsun pickup truck. They gave Walter six dollars and some change.

"You need this more than we do," said the father, wearing a mechanic's uniform, a streak of axle grease on his cheek. "God bless you."

"God bless you, too," said Walter, now with forty-eight dollars total.

On the crowded Greyhound bus, Walter vowed in his journal to find sobriety.

"I need to reclaim my life from drugs and alcohol," Walter wrote, sobbing. "I need to set an example for Lilly."

Hours later, Walter nearly fainted when he rounded the corner and saw two police cruisers parked in front of the Shady Acres Motel. Two uniformed Lakehaven cops chatted outside the door. One of the officers checked his watch while the other adjusted his sunglasses.

A paranoid-stricken Walter turned around and dashed to the bus stop at the end of the block.

--

The bus took him north to the Seattle Homeless Haven. In exchange for a hot dinner, he volunteered on the soup line, ladling bowl after steamy bowl of organic chicken stock with locally grown veggies and gluten-free noodles.

A rotation of gourmet grocers, including Searchlight columnist Alberto "The Whole Enchilada" Morales, donated soup all week, everything from chicken noodle to split pea. A nearby bakery set aside its surplus rolls, which were always soft and speckled with flour.

Walter became a regular at the shelter, with a nightly cot and hot bowl of soup. He found motels whenever he could afford an hour or two with a Craigslist hooker. Anything to get his mind off the guilt and shame of failure. Lilly seemed to ignore Walter's messages and letters. That rejection nauseated him more than the pills.

At night, amid the snoring men at the shelter, Walter ached for his daughter more than he ached for pills. He cried for her, wanted to hold her like a football, just like when she was a newborn. A silent teardrop rolled down his black cheek.

Walter slept on his back, blankets pulled up to his chin, white cap covering his face. He fantasized about a bed with box springs in a home where family life was the rule and love was unconditional.

He thought of his father's disappointed face.

"I will make you proud, Pops," Walter whispered to himself. "I will make you proud."

In the morning, after a restless night, the newly sober Walter hunted for pills and his book.

Star of the show

Pound! Pound! Pound!

Walter knocked with armageddon intensity.

Joe rubbed away his eye crust as he sprang out of bed.

Pound! Pound! Pound!

Joe stepped into his black loafers and slid his feet toward the front door, fresh out of REM sleep.

Pound! Pound! Pound!

Joe yanked the door open.

"Are you trying to wake up the whole goddamn neighborhood?"

"I knocked at the front door, just like you asked."

"Come in," said Joe, shuffling into the kitchen and starting the coffee maker. It had been weeks since they last saw each other. Bitter energy lingered in the air. They stood at opposite ends of the kitchen.

"Joe, I lost the book."

"What do you mean you lost the book? You show that thing to everyone like it's the Hope Diamond."

"My first speaking engagement is Friday at the library. Ernest Handsy has the only other copy."

"Call Ernest and borrow it. He might even let you keep it. For Christ's sake, you two quarrel like a couple of playground sissies."

"I am figuratively and literally blackballed at The Searchlight."

"I'm not getting caught up in your drama."

"He'll listen to you. Ask him if you can borrow the book," said Walter, clasping his hands. "Please."

"All right. I'll ask him. Next time I see him."

"I need the book by Friday."

"I'll call him after I eat breakfast," said Joe, rubbing his nose and face, glancing at the clock. It was noon.

Joe filled a pair of red coffee mugs to the brim. They both drank it black. Walter thanked Joe for agreeing to look for the book.

"Joe, this is important, especially for my daughter," said Walter, who walked out the front door and down the concrete steps, holding his chin up.

Joe opened the refrigerator and uncorked a half-full bottle of discount red wine. The "Jeopardy" theme song blared on the TV as he lounged on the couch and pondered his to-do list for the day.

Joe resented The Searchlight for the endorsement, and refused to acknowledge the newspaper. He had canceled his subscription on the day the endorsement was published, and had the only house on the street without a paper in the driveway every morning.

In considering Walter's request, Joe swallowed more than his pride. The call, if he made it, would signal an olive branch, which meant reuniting with Walter's tornado tendencies.

Joe finished the wine and dialed the newspaper.

(Outgoing message) "Hello, you've reached the desk of Ernest Handsy, editor of The Lakehaven Searchlight, your source for local news, opinions and sports. Please leave your name and number, and I will return your call as soon as possible. Thank you for reading The Searchlight." (automated voice: "Record your message after the tone.") (beep)

Joe pursed his lips, rolled his eyes, exhaled and hung up.

The next day, Walter left five voice messages for Joe about the book's status. On Friday morning, Walter waited at a nearby park until he was sure Joe was awake. To pass the time, he leafed through The Searchlight while seated on a bench.

He walked along the fir-lined suburban sidewalks. The cool salty breeze caressed his skin. A garden-gloved woman clipped hedges in her front yard, glaring as Walter passed.

Joe's house and empty driveway came into view. He pounded on the door and peeked in the window. Nobody home. Hot and thirsty from walking, Walter squatted by the coiled green garden hose. He twisted the faucet knob and drank from a skinny stream of mineral-heavy water, gasping for breath in between slurps.

He sat on Joe's concrete porch step to rest. Less than two minutes later, a police car pulled up. The officer, wearing sunglasses, got out of his car and held up his palm, signaling Walter to remain seated.

"We got a call about a man fitting your description peeping in windows. May I see your identification?"

Walter handed over his state ID card, which was acceptable for those without a driver's license - or in his case, those who had their driver's license revoked. The officer told Walter to wait while he conducted a background check. His heart pounded. The image of Mr. Hudson's crushed nose triggered a panic attack that whipped Walter's head and veins with hot flashes. His mind then flashed to the hotel shower arrest as the officer returned with Walter's identification.

"I thought I recognized you," the officer said. "I love your column. And between you and me, that racist officer is the bad apple in the bunch. We were all ashamed of how he treated you at the Paragon Hotel."

"Thank you, officer," Walter said with the world's driest

mouth and throat.

"I haven't seen your column in a while," the officer continued. "Do you still write for The Searchlight?"

"Not anymore," Walter said. "I had something going at the Seattle Daily News."

"Sounds like a step up," the officer said.

"I suppose."

"I'm glad somebody's got the guts to tell it like it is and go to bat for our kids."

"I do it with love."

Two miles later, Walter trudged into the library restroom, sweaty as a farmer. Two fliers hung on the bulletin board above the urinal. One flier urged library patrons to order their materials online. The other flier showed Walter's face and a picture of the book cover, plain white with large capital letters in Times New Roman font. His speaking engagement began in four hours. This was what the flier said:

"Telling it like it is: Lakehaven's education crisis," by Walter Wadsworth, local columnist for The Searchlight. Author reading begins at 7 p.m. Friday in the conference room at Lakehaven Regional Library.

Walter crumpled the flier after peeling it off the wall with a clawed hand. He tossed the paper in the garbage, pulled two white pills from his front pocket and washed them down with a drink from the sink. Twenty minutes later, Walter boarded a mid-afternoon bus for an impromptu trip to Spokane. He would return to Lakehaven one more time.

--

Walter's perspiration hit full force by the time he reached Spokane. The painkillers coursed through his veins and took the edge off his aching muscles.

He went to Spokane despite court orders that forbade unsupervised contact with Lilly until he underwent a psychiatric evaluation. The court also banned him from going anywhere near Rose.

Lilly had joined a ballet studio in Spokane. In her only letter since relocating, she mentioned her first performance. Walter devoted this day toward Lilly's show, starting with a bus ride. In his satchel - besides a stack of dirty Polaroids, half a fifth of whiskey and an orange bottle of pills - was an overdue library copy of "The Power of Positive Thinking." He thumbed through the first and fourth chapters, his favorites. He glanced out the bus window as the landscape morphed from rain forest to the high desert of Eastern Washington.

Almost three-hundred miles later, Walter exited near the Holiday Inn. It was dark and the recital started in 10 minutes. Lilly did not know Walter was coming. No one knew.

The theater was a mile away. The performance was under way when Walter wobbled into the empty lobby, which smelled like buttered popcorn. He watched from the back corner entrance, waiting for Lilly to take the stage. And there she was, leaping across the stage in pink slippers, her hair pulled into a bun, pink tights hugging her thick legs. She swayed to the symphony soundtrack, fanned her elegant fingers, posed like a glass ballerina. The silver sequins on her plus-size pink costume twinkled in the stage lights. Her eyes shined like diamonds.

Lilly was enrolled in her school's gifted program, to which Walter claimed credit. Walter imagined Lilly as a successful grown-up with an Ivy League degree. In these mind movies, the reason she grew up to be so beautiful and successful was because he had protected and nurtured her.

Lilly's feminine grace mesmerized Walter. As she danced, Walter remembered when she was a baby, when he called her his little football. Walter wanted to hold his football, to keep her all to himself. He thought of the nights when, as a baby, Lilly had a fever or a double ear infection. He held her and rocked with her through the night, dozing when she did. At that age, she slept best when Walter held her like a football, snug in the bend of his arm, every inch of her sealed in his safety. He thought of holding his little football one more time as they ran together, past the defenders and toward the goal-posts, their captors left behind to shrink as Walter and Lilly ran ahead.

"That's my girl," he whispered to himself as the music crescendoed to a climax. Lilly whirled with perfection in her bit part. The tiny dancer put tears in her father's eyes.

Lilly's Swan Lake scene ended with a modest curtsy and polite applause. A tear rolled down Walter's cheek. He turned his back to the wall and slid to the floor as his knees buckled. The applause drowned out his whimpering.

"Sir?" said a woman in a red vest, who touched his shoulder. "Are you all right?"

She was a volunteer usher. Her question, voiced in the quiet gap after the applause, caught the attention of nearby audience members. One of those people was Rose, whose glare locked with Walter's glazed eyes. She motioned to another usher to call the police, whispering to the usher about a restraining order.

The commotion halted the show. The orchestra, dancers and audience gawked. Walter backed toward the exit and saw Lilly at stage right, half concealed by the red curtain. Blinded by the stagelights, she shielded her eyes and saw a handful of people huddled at the theater door, blocking her view of the action.

Walter saw his daughter with a peekaboo view above the sea of heads.

"How long can I look at my baby girl before you force me

out?" Walter asked.

The wall of ushers in red vests moved in lockstep like a six-headed monster toward Walter, reducing the space between the exit. Walter's heart raced. He avoided eye contact with the human wall of red vests. His gaze was locked on the girl he had rocked to sleep while holding her like a football.

The wall of red vests repeated: "Sir, please leave."

By the time he pushed the exit doors open, Walter had lost his peekaboo view of Lilly. He stood in the doorway and pointed toward the stage.

"That's my girl up there. Star of the show," he said, backing out the door. "Star of the show."

His heart pumped into overdrive. Fifteen minutes later, he boarded a Greyhound back to Seattle.

The show resumed moments after Walter left the building.

"Whew! That could have turned ugly," said one usher.

"Who was that guy?"

"I don't know, but man, he needed a shower."

"He sure was out of it."

"He was drunk as a skunk."

"Who was that guy?"

"I don't know, some lady in there told me to call the police because her stalker showed up."

"Who the hell was that guy?"

"Relax, he was just a random crazy bum."

The whole enchilada

Later at the Seattle Homeless Haven, Alberto "The Whole Enchilada" Morales ladled his trademark tortilla soup, the same soup that cost his customers seven dollars a bowl: tender shredded chicken with handmade corn tortilla triangles bathed in a bold cumin-streaked broth. The men at the shelter loved how the soup made their noses runny. "Cures what ails you," they said.

He volunteered Sunday nights at the shelter with a crew of hair-netted churchmates who spoke a dual-language soundtrack. Morales donated the entire package, from food to labor, and even stocked the refrigerators with enough leftover soup for Monday.

The satisfied slurps of the hungry men echoed in the dining hall. The soup warmed their bones.

On this night, Morales added mini enchiladas to the menu. Served on red plastic saucers, the enchiladas were model versions of his restaurant's signature dish, The Whole Enchilada, bursting with beef and cheddar cheese, drizzled with red and green salsas.

With dark circles under his bloodshot eyes, Walter waited with his tray and empty bowl. He had grown tired of sleeping on a bus. He needed a bed and a hot meal. He wilted like a plant without water. He missed his daughter.

"Walter, how you doing, man?" said Morales, whose column still ran in The Searchlight. "Long time, no see. I haven't seen your column in a while. What happened, amigo?"

"It's a long story," Walter mumbled, handing over his bowl. He wanted to trade places with The Whole Enchilada and run a restaurant, feed the homeless, write a column, and tuck his child into bed every night.

On this day, Morales also delivered two-hundred pairs of heavy-duty cotton socks, thanks to a deal with the boss at the Hanes factory. Walter stuffed two pairs of socks into his satchel.

He knew several shelter clients from the all-night bus. Some were as smart as Walter and plagued with more demons. Walter befriended everyone from an aerospace engineer-turned-junkie to a shell-shocked Marine who served two tours in Iraq.

As he stood up to take his tray to the sink, a sharp pain stabbed his arm from shoulder to wrist. He hobbled toward a wall, leaning against it, gasping for breath.

"You feeling OK?" Morales called out while rinsing soup bowls in scalding hot water. "Do you need a doctor?"

"I'm fine," Walter said, measuring his speech, moving his bent arm in a slow windmill. "Arthritis. No big deal. Cold weather aggravates it. That's all."

Morales shook his hands dry, walked up and place his palm on Walter's shoulder. His piercing brown eyes were filled with genuine concern.

"I'm not trying to get in your business, amigo, but you look dead tired."

"If you were homeless," Walter said, "you'd look dead tired, too."

Walter limped to his cot and thumbed through the journal entry from that morning. Scratched in blue ink, he wrote about a dream that starred his father. The rest of the day, with the dream swirling in his mind, Walter planned the next morning's journal entry as a pledge to be a better parent to Lilly. Walter always said that Lilly showed him the light - that she was the light of his world.

The day of Lilly's birth and the moments before her first cry, as a brand new human on this planet, was the most emotional experience of Walter's life. The meaning of life had become clear: he would have given his own life, no questions asked, if it meant his daughter would live.

"I finally caught my breath when Lilly took her first breath," Walter wrote in his journal. "Since then, I have never been the same."

The shelter's overhead lights dimmed to dark. Walter folded his hands upon his chest. He dozed, smiling in silence at the memory of kissing Lilly's cheeks and squeezing her hands. He relaxed, self-assured of a second chance. He vowed to make it count. He drifted to sleep for the final time, a white hat resting upon his face, a mortal man who died after finding peace from the promise of one more sunrise.

Walter's last journal entry

I usually don't remember my dreams, but I had the strangest dream of my life this morning.

I saw Pops, off in the distance, silhouetted by the setting sun along the horizon. He turned around and disappeared out of sight. I ran my hardest to catch up to him, calling for him with all my might: "I'm not afraid!"

Pops only said, "I know. Follow the light." That's all he would say. I never heard my father say "follow the light" like some kind of Socrates clone.

We rode one of those speedy walkways you'd find at the airport terminal. Each terminal was a movie scene of sorts. One terminal showed young men in army helmets, holding big rifles, backs against a dirt wall, deafened by the explosive soundtrack of war. Most of their platoon was dead, the bodies scattered and bloodied. Standing next to me on the walkway, I stared at Pops as he watched himself in this scene, where he was a young sergeant leading a handful of young soldiers. It was life or death.

"On my command, charge with your bayonet and scream like wild Indians!" the young Pops shouted over the mortar blasts and gunfire. "Shoot from the hip!"

The Americans charged enemy gunfire with primal rage as

the enemy fled.

The walkway shifted to a terminal that smelled like buttered popcorn and aftershave. It felt like being at the movies with Pops. I remembered the way he laughed. The movie screen showed a younger Pops hitting baseballs to me, one after the other. Then the bat became a golf club, but he's still hitting baseballs. I caught every ball.

In the next scene, a fat detective with a fu-manchu mustache put handcuffs on me. The walkway brought Pops, myself and the detective to the next terminal, which was dark. I told Pops I hadn't seen him in a while. He talked about the weather like he always did: "Oh, we've been getting a lot of rain lately. It was 82 degrees Saturday, and the next thing you know, it's 62 degrees on Sunday. Either way, I've got to mow the lawn before it rains."

With the detective out of the picture, I told my father I wished we saw each other more.

"I know," he said. "Follow the light."

"This is a long walkway and all this beer makes me have to pee," I told him, suddenly with a can of Rainier beer in each hand as we moved on the walkway. "I'll either pee or wake up, and I'd much prefer to pee."

"I know," he said. "Follow the light."

I stepped off the walkway, alone in the dark. I walked into a three-walled terminal, suddenly blinded by nuclear-strength light. It was a sterile hospital room with Pops in the bed. A bed on the other side of the room was empty.

He drooled in bed, doped up on painkillers. He always refused medicine, even when healthy. That's when I knew the end was getting close. The mashed potatoes and glazed gravy had cooled to room temperature atop a tray next to the bed.

"Do you like your lunch?" I asked him.

"No." He barely spoke above a whisper. He was never a loud man, but he never sounded so weak. In this scene, he couldn't move or speak at all. He was dying. It was just me and my father in the all-white room with all-white walls.

"I love you."

"I know," he said. I said "I love you" again. Men from his generation never said I love you to boys or men.

It would have meant everything to hear him say that to me, if only in a dream.

"You'll always be my pal, and I'll always be your pal," I said, tears rolling down my cheeks.

"I know." He puckered his lips and made a kissing sound. I hesitated. His pale peeling lips had a ring of dried food around them. He puckered his lips again to ask for a kiss. I leaned forward and lightly kissed his lips, a small peck.

"You will always be my hero."

"I know. Follow the light."

That's all I can remember from the dream. Pops, if you can read this from up in Heaven, I want you to know that to this day, when faced with a decision, I ask, what would you do? Sometimes you're wrong, and sometimes I'm right. In the end, I know that every morning you woke up, you were grateful to live another day.

I feel the same way, Pops. I will make you proud. I will be the best man and father I can be. I will follow the light.

The obituaries

"For every peak, there is a valley," Walter once wrote. "Every soul has its seasons. It's a shame the seasons come and go so fast."

Alongside Walter's fall from grace, Joe Lippy made good on his promise to drop out of civic life, although he occasionally ventured to the grocery store, swerving in the pea green Cadillac, puffing on that pipe, a tweed fedora cupping his gray mad scientist hair.

Several months had passed since Joe saw Walter after closing the proverbial door and convincing himself it was for the best. Joe also knew Walter was a stain who never fully faded away.

Clad in a terry cloth robe and black slippers on a sunny afternoon with a wine hangover, Joe answered a persistent knock at the door. A state employee was looking for Walter's next of kin. Minutes later, he dialed Ernest at The Searchlight.

"Ernest, it's Joe Lippy."

"Joe, long time no talk to. How are you?"

"Walter died."

"What? When?"

"I found the obituary in the Seattle Daily News. He died last month at a homeless shelter in Seattle. The obit said he died of unknown causes."

"I bet his demons finally caught up."

"I'm sure it had something to do with his pill habit," Joe said. "Damned if I know."

"I thought you two were friends?"

"For a while, he was out of my life, thank God. He was like a hungry cat who stayed where he was fed. What a parasite. No more borrowing money, no more mooching rides, no more random knocks at my window," Joe said. "For a while he was sleeping in my car. Did you know about that? I refused to loan him more money after he wrecked the car, you see."

"I'll call the medical examiner's office and find out the official cause of death."

"Yes, that's a good idea. Would you do me favor and call me when you find out?"

"Of course. I'll write something up today. Walter had some hardcore fans."

"I know," Joe said, eyes watering. "I know."

That afternoon, Joe and Ernest continued the conversation at a Chinese buffet in downtown Lakehaven. Their plates steamed with mounds of fried rice and spicy chicken.

"Whatever happened to Walter's book?" Joe asked with a mouthful of food. "He carried that book around like it was the Hope Diamond and showed it to everybody, and I mean everybody, even to strangers in public restrooms. One day, I asked him about the book, and he said he lost it. He wanted me to hit you up for the other copy."

"The printer sent two copies as proofs before going out of business. I gave mine to some random woman who asked me about it. I trashed all the files too. I just wanted to wash my hands clean of his shit, if you know what I mean."

"That's too bad. I bet that book could make a lot of money," Joe said. "Have you talked to his daughter?"

"About the book?"

"About the book and her father."

"Does his daughter know that he died?" Ernest asked. "Lilly, I think, is her name."

"I'm sure she'll find out when she reads the obituary."

"Love him or hate him, everyone in Lakehaven would read him," Ernest said, shaking his head. "He came across like such a distinguished gentleman in that column. If the readers only knew the real Walter."

"He leveraged that column to borrow money from just about everyone in Lakehaven. They were all pissed that he never paid them back. I loaned him, let's see, probably two-thousand dollars total, and he never paid me back."

"Not to mention all the time and energy he sapped from my daily life."

"If you can find that book, The Searchlight can earn some of that money back," Joe said. "Doesn't the paper own the rights?"

"Walter had some exception in his freelance contract. I'd have to refresh my memory on the terms again," said Ernest, who shoved his empty rice-flecked plate to the edge of the table a few minutes after Joe did the same. They cycled the buffet for second plates, each piled high with rice, crab rangoon, kung pao chicken and egg rolls.

"I can't believe I miss that son of a bitch," Joe said, pouring soy sauce all over his food.

"I know. For someone who annoyed me so much, I'm slightly sad that he's gone."

"He was a character," Joe said, hands folded on the table, eyes glazed by the light from the floor-to-ceiling windows. His eyes glistened for a microsecond before he said those words again. "He was a character."

Walter's obituary ran on the front page under the headline "Former columnist dies homeless." Alberto "The Whole Enchilada" Morales, the trusty food columnist, had volunteered at the homeless shelter the night Walter died.

"He'd been staying here, regularly, for at least three months, maybe longer," Morales told Ernest. "Walter constantly talked about his daughter and how proud he was of her. He was planning to move to Spokane at the end of the month so that he could see her every day. He would say things like, 'I was put on this Earth to be her father.' You could tell that the distance between them took a toll on his well-being."

According to the county medical examiner, Walter died of a heart attack. Morales said one shelter guest had heard Walter making strange noises in his sleep that night. In the morning, the shelter guests had crowded around Walter, waiting for the ambulance. One man folded Walter's hands atop his chest and straightened the white cap over his face.

--

The city hosted its annual ceremony for homeless people who had died in the past year. The public appreciated the sentimental gesture. Tucked in a green nook of Lakehaven Memorial Cemetery was a plain horizontal granite slab with the epitaph "Gone but not forgotten, these beautiful people of Lakehaven." These same beautiful people had been cremated and sifted into individual cardboard boxes, then finally discarded if their remains went unclaimed.

A small crowd surrounded the forest green camping tent staked across the gravestone for the homeless.

Half the people in the crowd wore black jackets with the county medical examiner's logo. A range of leaders from the faith community waited in line for their turn to speak. A rabbi straightened his yarmulke. A priest crossed himself. A Native American chaplain fidgeted with an eagle feather and a cigarette lighter, rehearsing a prayer in his native tongue.

The burial honored forty-four homeless people, seven of whom were women. The county chaplain, with a twinkling gold cross pinned to his uniform, recited the list of names.

"On this day, the dead are teaching us a lesson in life," he said at the podium, voice crackling through portable speakers. He held up a self-portrait by a deceased black artist who was nicknamed Teeth because of his beaver-like incisors.

Ernest stood with the rest of the media, which included two nightly news stations that documented the ceremony. The Seattle Daily News assigned a photographer, who swaggered with thousands of dollars in camera gear around his neck and shoulders. The clicks of his camera augmented the silence and prayer.

"All go to the same place (click), all come from dust (click), and to dust all return," said the chaplain, reading from Ecclesiastes as the shutterbug worked the scene. "There is a time for everything (click click), and a season for every activity (click) under heaven ..."

Behind the TV cameramen stood a dozen living homeless people who watched from the back, wiping tears from their faces.

"Good people pass away (click), but the godly often die (click) before their time," said the priest, sprinkling holy water on the headstone and the crouching photographer.

To conclude the ceremony, the medical examiner and his deputy recited the list of forty-four people who died poor and destitute. For a moment, Ernest thought they skipped Walter. He double-checked the list, then later confirmed with the county that Walter's remains had been claimed by "next of kin," according to the file. The ceremony at the cemetery honored the paupers whose remains went unclaimed within three weeks of death.

Ernest learned that Walter's ashes had been boxed and shipped to Los Angeles. His brother, Harold Wadsworth, bought a football-sized urn and displayed the ashes on a nightstand in a spare bedroom. Ernest tracked down that scrap of paper Walter had given him last year and called Harold. A man with a deep voice answered.

"I saw the obituary you wrote," Harold said. "Thank you."

Ernest said that several community members had asked about a memorial and wondered if anything was planned to honor Walter.

Harold sounded annoyed. "I loved my brother and I'm sorry that he's gone. We had a love-hate relationship. We were at odds for years over our personal beliefs. His life was a mess. Thank God his ex-wife got custody of their daughter."

"Is there anything missing in the obituary, or anything you'd like to add?"

"No," he answered after a pause.

"Walter also wrote a book. Only two copies were printed, and I can't find either."

"If you find the book or come across anything that belonged to him, please call me," said Harold, and hung up.

None of Walter's belongings ever turned up, like that book, or the brown satchel, or the pinstripe suit. Maybe the medical examiner included Walter's white cap with his ashes. He left behind more than debts and a daughter. He had given birth to 142 pages worth of newspaper columns, bound with a generic black and white cover, and written with love.

--

Walter's death plastered a grin on Rose. She was addicted to hating him. His ghost haunted her life in Lakehaven, whether in the newspaper or through the gossip mill or from the traits Lilly inherited from her father.

Lilly learned from The Searchlight's obituary that her father died. That's also when Lilly learned her father was homeless. Grandma had clipped the article and mailed it to Rose and Lilly in Spokane. Rose was angry that Lilly had written a letter to the newspaper in response.

Camped on a stool by the open kitchen window with a smoldering cigarette, Rose dialed Ernest at The Searchlight.

"My daughter wrote you a letter about her father's obituary," she said. "Please don't print that. I didn't approve of her writing that letter in the first place."

"I'm sorry to learn she lost her father. Walter was an interesting man."

"Are you kidding me? He was a con artist. That column you guys printed week after week? Pure bullshit."

"A lot of readers liked him," Ernest said.

"He was a hypocrite," Rose said. "He wrote about being a good father when his own daughter never saw a dime in child support. Not one dime."

"I hadn't planned on printing Lilly's letter, so no worries."

"I noticed the paper had stopped running his column. You finally wised up."

"Long story short, he was causing trouble in the community," Ernest said. "He was a suffocating presence."

"I feel bad that Lilly lost her father, but their relationship was dying on the vine," she said. "All I know is that, dead or alive, Walter is a curse."

Ernest also felt cursed by the living and dead versions of Walter. If he was stuck with Walter's ghost, he was going to make it pay.

He needed to find that book. He called every secondhand bookstore and combed the county's libraries. No leads.

That night, with a glass of wine and his children asleep upstairs in his middle-class home, Ernest sat at the kitchen table under the dimmed-light of a brass chandelier. With a blue pen and spiral notebook, Ernest wrote a letter to the ghost of the most brilliant homeless father in Lakehaven history.

Dear Walter,

You're haunting me as I write this. I always learned from you. The day the paper cut you off was one of the most liberating days of my career. A weight was lifted from my shoulders. I felt smothered by you. I appreciated your intelligence and talent. You overshadowed those gifts when you took the status the newspaper gave you and used it for ill gain.

I naturally keep people at a distance. I need that personal space. You mistook my kindness for weakness. You exploited my good nature, the kind of good nature that everyone deserves and, if they want, can steal.

I took you in when the rest of the world said no. I got repaid with poison and greed. The Searchlight lifted your crown of thorns and defended you to every honcho in the city who wanted to take you down. You won the minds and hearts of the regular folks. These are the non-engaged members of the public, the ones who wisely avoid politics. They live free of the drama. They channel their energies toward survival. They eat, sleep, pray and play. Several behave like you behind closed motel doors.

Walter, I believed in your gifts. I polished your jagged diamond. Why couldn't you just behave?

You merged into daily life at the newspaper. I had no choice but to accept your presence. And I figured, if I have to put up with you, I might as well get something out of you. In your case, you wanted higher status. To keep it, you had to put up with me.

You were an exciting presence for an otherwise passive social life. I rarely choose my friends, therefore, I accept the friends who choose me. You chose me, burned me, and I cut the umbilical cord. It was all for the best.

I am sad that your time at the paper, and on this planet, came to a dead end. You died a pauper, but you were never poor. My only regret is not taking you more seriously. Then again, you didn't make it easy. As you once wrote, life is simple, but people are complicated.

Rest in peace, my reluctant friend.

Yours truly,

Ernest Handsy

--

That night, on the other side of Lakehaven, in the corner of his crowded room, Joe Lippy and his .44 Magnum were fully loaded.

On his desk sat two empty bottles of merlot, a wrinkled copy of The Searchlight, and a bumper sticker from his school board campaign. He opened the bedroom window to let in the breeze through the screen. He heard a loose redwood pine cone hit the lawn with a muffled thud. In the quiet room, a shirtless Joe polished the .44-Magnum beneath the hot light of a desk lamp. The next morning, he was going to the gun range with a new friend.

Without warning, a mouse trap snapped. Joe gasped and turned toward a dresser. He strapped a tan leather holster around his bare shoulder, the white strap running through his gray-haired chest. He looked in the mirror, admiring the machismo and danger of concealing a weapon like a secret agent. One more piece, and the fantasy in the mirror was complete. Still gazing in the mirror, he leaned over and groped for the gun, gripping it by the barrel.

The gun slipped out of his hand and fell to the floor. The eardrum-shattering shot woke up his girlfriend and the neighbors. The last thing Joe saw was a flash from the barrel.

Three days later, The Searchlight published his obituary. Word traveled through the rumor mill that Joe's girlfriend had the body cremated, as he requested. The silver urn was filled with Joe's ashes and rested on the desk, next to his pipe, bathed by light from the same window where his friend Walter always knocked.

Walter's searchlight

Children in backpacks and parents with cameras crowded around the front entrance of the newly remodeled Mount Rainier Elementary School.

The mid-August breeze graced the school's dedication ceremony beneath cotton-cloud blue skies and chirping sparrows. A few old-growth evergreens shaded the entrances at the traditional red brick campus, which had a fresh-mowed grass aroma. The blacktopped basketball court reflected the morning sunlight, with nets dangling from unbent rims attached to unscratched fiberglass backboards. In a sea of wood chips was a yellow and blue jungle gym with slides, bridges and monkey bars. The brown box benches had an inscription, noting they were made from recycled plastic. Sprinklers misted the landscape into golf course green at a time when most lawns went brown from the dry Northwest summer.

Missing from the school was Lilly Wadsworth, who had moved to Spokane, and Walter Wadsworth, who no longer waited across the courtyard for his daughter.

A yellow ribbon spanned the entrance to the school. Lakehaven's most famous politician, Levi Cooke, emerged from the gang of elected officials who crowded for a photo-friendly position behind the yellow ribbon. Ernest concurrently observed The Searchlight intern, whose camera clicked away as the dignitaries spoke.

"Ladies and gentlemen (click), thank you for joining us today as we (click click) dedicate the new Mount Rainier Elementary School," Cooke announced with the superintendent by his side. The intern snapped photos from both sides of the ribbon.

"Before we cut this ribbon," Cooke said, "I'd like to take a moment to recognize one of Lakehaven's most colorful education advocates, Walter Wadsworth, who recently passed away in a homeless shelter."

The crowd fell silent.

"Anyone who cared about education in Lakehaven knew about Walter and his column in The Searchlight (click). He and I did not always see eye to eye (click)," Cooke said. "But I always respected his genuine concern (click) and passion (click) for arming Lakehaven's students with the tools they need to succeed in life (click). Before I was elected to be your state representative, I had the honor and privilege of teaming with Walter to improve our schools. One of my favorite memories is the time we oversaw the installation of video monitors and digital overhead projectors in each classroom at Mount Rainier Elementary. Since then, the school's test scores have improved forty percent."

The crowd roared with applause before Cooke continued.

"Lakehaven's parents can thank Walter for his advocacy on behalf of their children (click). Walter shined his light not on us, but in us, and Lakehaven schools are better because of him. Now let's make him proud."

The crowd applauded. Cooke gestured for Superintendent Harvey Oakes to come forward and speak. The superintendent took the microphone and faced the students and parents before him.

"I am also saddened by Walter's passing. Lakehaven

schools will ensure (click) that no child is left behind. As Walter once said, an education that is earned is an education that is kept (click). You, the students, will earn that education and live a better life."

He waited for the applause to subside.

"You, the parents, will give this school dignity. We the community will leave a legacy, and that will be a legacy born out of love for the children." He paused. "Thank you, Lakehaven, for standing up and demanding more for our children. It's up to us. Let's get busy."

Amid the cheers, the superintendent steadied the giant scissors. Cooke stood to his left, next to esteemed school board member Ted Farley. Peeking from the back row was Geoffrey Parker, who donated coffee and doughnuts for the event. Parker stood next to the school's gym teacher, Mr. Hudson, who smiled with new front teeth and fuzzy memories of his assault in a secluded bathroom.

The Searchlight's intern steadied his camera for the front page photo.

"Ladies and gentlemen, students and parents, and the entire community of Lakehaven, I present to you, the new and improved Mount Rainier Elementary School."

The scissors snapped, the ribbon fell, the people clapped. Adults shook hands, parents hugged children, and students streamed through the front door.

Ernest drove back to the office in his Jeep with the windows open and the day's news on his mind. While waiting at a stoplight, a pedestrian in the crosswalk caught his eye - a black man with a white cap, swinging his arms in stride. He looked a lot like Walter, only about fifty pounds heavier. Walter's doppelganger paused, locked eyes with Ernest, flashed a toothy smile and resumed his gait. Ernest grinned, and when the stoplight turned from red to green, he drove forward.

--

Meanwhile, on the opposite side of the Cascade mountains, some three-hundred miles away in a two-bedroom condo, Lilly awaited her first day at a new middle school.

The Spokane forecast called for high temperatures in the mid-seventies all week, with partly cloudy skies and a fifty percent chance of rain.

Rose nudged open Lilly's door. The sun shined through venetian blinds, casting a striped pattern on her daughter, who was awake in bed.

"Rise and shine, dear," said Rose, clutching her bathrobe closed. "I'm going to blow-dry my hair and then I'll fix you some eggs. Sound good?"

Lilly nodded and Rose shuffled to the bathroom. With Rose's roaring hairdryer in the distance, Lilly leaped out of bed. She loaded her pink vinyl backpack with two plain green folders, a spiral notebook, a black pen and a box of pencils. Into the backpack went a teddy bear with matted blue fur, loose stitches and a missing button eye. Lilly had slept with the teddy bear since her toddler years, forgoing a name for the bear and simply referring to the plush toy for what it was.

The thought of the teddy bear in her backpack was comforting. It eased the jitters of attending a school where she knew only herself.

"Lilly, eggs will be ready in a minute. Go wash up," Rose hollered from the kitchen, clanging a skillet.

"I'm packing my school supplies. I'll be right there."

"Hurry up," Rose said. "I don't want you to miss the school bus."

Across from Lilly's bed was a bookcase with two shelves, standing belly high. With her index finger, she pulled out the skinny book with white binding and black lettering. The book occupied the first spot on the top shelf.

184

She opened the front cover, as she did every day, and smiled at the words written in black ink on the first page:

"This book is dedicated to Lilly Wadsworth, the light of my life. Love, Daddy."

Lilly tucked the book next to the teddy bear and zipped the backpack closed.

Made in the USA
Lexington, KY
04 December 2013